ALEXANDER'S RELATIONS

ALEXANDER'S RELATIONS

Roger Stokes

Copyright © 2022 Roger Stokes

The moral right of the author has been asserted.

Apart from any fair dealing for the purposes of research or private study, or criticism or review, as permitted under the Copyright, Designs and Patents Act 1988, this publication may only be reproduced, stored or transmitted, in any form or by any means, with the prior permission in writing of the publishers, or in the case of reprographic reproduction in accordance with the terms of licences issued by the Copyright Licensing Agency. Enquiries concerning reproduction outside those terms should be sent to the publishers.

This is a work of fiction. Names, characters, businesses, places, events and incidents are either the products of the author's imagination or used in a fictitious manner. Any resemblance to actual persons, living or dead, or actual events is purely coincidental.

Matador
Unit E2 Airfield Business Park,
Harrison Road, Market Harborough,
Leicestershire. LE16 7UL
Tel: 0116 2792299
Email: books@troubador.co.uk
Web: www.troubador.co.uk/matador
Twitter: @matadorbooks

ISBN 978 1803130 903

British Library Cataloguing in Publication Data.
A catalogue record for this book is available from the British Library.

Printed and bound in the UK by TJ Books LTD, Padstow, Cornwall
Typeset in 11pt Acumin Pro by Troubador Publishing Ltd, Leicester, UK

Matador is an imprint of Troubador Publishing Ltd

For
Sam, Jack, Luc, Ruby, Ronnie,
Oscar, Poppy and Maggie

ONE

2007 – MARCUS

I'm leaning against one of those old London plane trees outside Holland Park Tube, waiting for Dave to arrive.

To while away the time, I take a look at the people sitting outside the Starbucks next to the station. It's one of those early days in June– the kind of day when it's not as warm as it looks and you wish you'd worn a sweater – and quite a few tables are occupied, although the appeal of the tables is more to do with smoking than good weather. There's the usual array of yummy mummies – posh clothes, posh accents, sunglasses pushed up onto glossy hair – chatting to each other, idly pushing a baby buggy to and fro with one bored hand. A group of younger girls hang out together, probably foreign language students. They look identical – slim, blonde, dressed unfashionably in pale blue jeans and tight crop tops revealing several inches of smooth flesh above the hip bone – don't they ever feel cold? – and the inevitable navel piercing, meaning there's usually a tattoo not far away, smoking furiously as they wave their hands and gabble away in some eastern European language or text on their mobiles, thumbs moving at impressive speed. They are oblivious to any passing male conditioned to check them out, drawn like a magnet to their undeniable youth and good looks.

I've never liked Starbucks. I don't like the American gung-ho jollity, I don't like the giant mugs (what's wrong with a cup?), and I certainly don't like the weak, beige-coloured, too-hot brew they call coffee. I don't understand why it's become so popular. Maybe it's the free refills, the huge muffins, the chance to sit all day on one of the sofas that always seem to be occupied, usually by some tramp-like figure surrounded by carrier bags, or some pseud pretending to read a book and making notes like they're researching their latest novel.

How difficult can it be to make a decent cup of coffee? Ever since I returned from a trip down under, I've been on a mission to find a café that serves a flat white. Two shots of espresso into a nice warm round cup, hot milk poured slowly, tiny crema bubbles on top that descend as you drink the coffee, a little design on top reflecting the mood of the barista. How hard can that be? It will be several years before I find my flat white in a café, surprisingly, in Devon that employs a Kiwi, and then Costa will spread the good news nationwide, but that, as they say, is all in the future.

Dave emerges from the station, looks both ways then spots me against the tree.

'What-ho, Marcus,' says Dave, 'trying to look cool, are we?'

Apart from Dave, hardly anyone calls me Marcus. In the leafy suburb of Pinner where I was born, I don't recall there being another Marcus. My parents, Reg and Betty, good pre-war names, were not pretentious people. The story goes my mother had been reading one of her beloved history books and came across the name the day before she gave birth – it was just on her mind. So here I was, Marcus Kingsley, born and raised in Pinner, educated at the local grammar school. There, I was mostly "Marco", a name I grew to like even more as a teenager when I imagined it gave me something of a continental appeal. Later, when I was in the band, I would have more success with this image, although with my "classic" (to me) dirty blond, northern European looks, why any girl would mistake my Marco for a Latin eluded me, but then who knew what went through the mind of a slightly drunk teenage girl peering up at a sweat-soaked singer?

Dave and I start to walk down Holland Park Avenue (does anyone really know where the Avenue ends and Bayswater Road begins?), past the shop that sells newspapers from around the world, and London's most expensive butcher.

'Do you ever look at women in the street and wonder if they had sex last night?' says Dave.

It's a well-known fact in London that a very attractive woman will pass by – one you'd really like to meet and maybe spend the rest of your life with – every two and a half minutes. Like the girl approaching now. Slim body, confident stride, beautiful long, dark curly hair and skin the colour of coffee – real coffee, not Starbuck's beige. I'm thinking maybe she's Colombian (that's another good guessing game) and send her a smile which she returns with interest, revealing perfect white teeth. And then she's gone, and I'll never know what a perfect life we might have had.

'You need to get out more,' I reply. 'When was the last time you had sex?'

Dave goes quiet for a while. Being an honest soul, he needs to mull this over.

'When did we have that holiday in Brittany?'

'What? The one where you tried windsurfing?'

'Yeah, that one. I met a lovely Dutch lady in a bar that was playing dreadful French rock 'n' roll, and she took me back to her campervan. I think she might have been a bit pissed. I know I was. Probably drinking that Fockin' gin!'

We both laugh. Still smiling, I pat him gently on the back. 'That was at least six years ago, mate, probably more.'

'Oh well,' says Dave, 'doesn't time fly when you're having a good time? Fancy a pint?'

We turn into Princedale Road and head towards the Alfred. Inside, we make our way to the bar.

'Jesus, what happened to this place?' says Dave. I begin to think it was a mistake bringing Dave here. It used to be my local, but I stopped coming when it changed hands a couple of years ago. Sprouting from the bar is an array of metal pumps offering five different lagers, two ciders, three Belgian beers and Guinness, served ice cold. The guy behind the bar is not that interested in serving us, probably because we don't fit the "target profile" of the restaurant chain that now owns the pub. It's the sort of place where all the staff wear black trousers and t-shirts with the name of the pub embroidered in tiny script across the chest.

'So, what can I get you guys?' says t-shirt man. Dave and I look at each other.

'Got any draft bitter?' says Dave, hopefully. T-shirt guy looks at Dave as if he was wearing a flat cap and hobnailed boots, with string holding up his trousers.

'Not much call for that now, mate. I can do you a bottle of beer – German, French, Spanish, Italian, English?'

We settle on two – expensive – bottles of an organic regional English beer weirdly named "Hogs Back". The barman leaves my change in a small white dish which he places on the counter in front of me, presuming I might want to leave a tip for his customer-focussed service. Fuck off. As if.

It's still early so we find a table by the window, look around and shrug to each other at the lack of atmosphere in this pseudo- pub.

'Cheers anyway,' says Dave. 'Good to see you.' He takes a sip of his expensive organic regional English beer. 'Actually, not bad,' he admits, 'shame it's so bloody cold.'

Dave was, still is, I suppose, the drummer in our band, Alexander's Relations, named after Keith's family pet, a golden Labrador. Dave's a pretty good vocalist too, and we'd often harmonise together. At school, he was unbelievably bright, especially at physics and maths (funny how you read about musicians who are keen on science; why's that, do you think?) and later had a big job at the Met Office predicting storms, before he took a lucrative early retirement.

Dave gazes out of the window. I can see the question forming in his head: *How do such small houses sell for such big millions?* But the question he eventually asks is, 'Did you get Ali's invite?'

Alison's invitation. It arrived about ten days ago. A folded card with a black and white photo of a six-year-old Alison on the front and inside an invitation to her 60th birthday party, to be held at her and Keith's country pile in Sussex. Across the inside was a handwritten note: *The perfect time for a band reunion. How about it, xx?*

Jesus, it must be at least twenty years since we'd played together. Keith was throwing a fortieth birthday party for Alison and thought it would be a great idea if the band got back together to play some of the "old" songs (or more likely give Keith the chance to show off to his wealthy new friends that he used to be in a band). The whole thing had been a shambles. We arrived under-rehearsed, no one under thirty liked the music, Steve got high and fell off the, admittedly, small stage. And I ended up having a drunken shag in the garden shed with a sexy young girl who later turned out to be the "rebel" daughter of one of Keith's biggest clients. We all vowed there and then, never again.

Dave has finished his drink and is slowly shredding a beer mat.

'Come on,' I say, 'I'll take you to a proper pub with real ale then I'll cook you something to eat. We can talk about Alison's invite later.'

Dave's eyes light up at the thought of food. Living by himself and not much of a cook, he's firmly in the "eat to live, not live to eat" camp. We leave the Albert to its target profile of Malbec drinkers and gastro-pub clientele.

TWO

1965

'Hey, Sparko, are you lot playing tonight?'

Pete is shouting at me across the changing room. Sparko. It's a name I acquired a couple of years ago after a rugby match against some thugs from Hendon. During the match, their inside centre aimed a punch at me and as I ducked he caught me on the side of the head. I went down for a few seconds – I swear I wasn't knocked out – but the rest of the team said I was; so after that, I'd always been called "Sparko" instead of Marco.

I got my revenge later that night when I shagged his girlfriend in the car park. I'd stepped outside the clubhouse to get some fresh air and smoke a cigarette when she came out of the ladies and saw me. Short and a bit on the plump side, not my type really, but a pretty face and really nice tits. She stroked my bruised face; 'Would you like me to kiss that better?'

Within seconds, we were kissing furiously and she'd begun to pull me across the car park towards a car, her car (I think it was a Morris Minor, but I could be wrong). We were on the back seat, tights off, knickers off, trousers off and still locked at the lips. It was all over in a minute or two but intensely satisfying all the same.

'Thanks, that was really nice,' she said as we shared a cigarette. 'Sorry about my arsehole of a boyfriend. He thinks if he punches someone it will impress me.' Then she sorted herself out, climbed out of the car and sauntered back to the clubhouse, turning at the door to give me a wicked smile and a wink.

'Yes, Pete, we are indeed. Starts at eight. Is that gorgeous sister of yours coming?'

'If she does, she won't be coming anywhere near you, mate!' says Pete, and everyone laughs. The changing room is thick with the after-match smell of mud, wet towels, beer, cigarette smoke and fifteen blokes smothering themselves with talc and anything else they'd been given for Christmas in the mistaken belief it might make them more attractive to the opposite sex.

The rest of the band start arriving around seven. Alison and Steve are in their mum's Mini; keyboard, guitar and amp on the back seat. Keith and Dave pull up in Dave's old Land Rover, a highly impractical vehicle in the suburbs but big enough to swallow his drum kit and the rest of our gear.

After a couple of beers and a catch-up on news, we start to set up at one end of the large dining room that will become the dancefloor.

When the band got its first gig at the rugby club, I'd had to put up with a lot of laughing, whistling and some obscene, but friendly, advice when I started to sing. But people soon realised we could play, and my singing became less important than the music. We play songs to dance to – Beatles, Stones, Manfred Mann, Searchers, Animals, but not The Who (I could never reach the high notes of Daltry). I'd have loved to include some Tamla Motown, but you really needed horns for that, so I stick to singing and playing harmonica.

We always start with Booker T's *Green Onions* and segue into *House of the Rising Sun*. After twenty minutes or so, the room would usually be crowded with people dancing and singing along, and we could lose ourselves in the buzz and enjoyment of playing together.

Ali sits at the keyboard, head bent down, long hair swaying across her face like a curtain. She always takes off her glasses to play; that way, she reckons she can't see anyone in the audience and, bizarrely, believes they can't see her. I've fancied Ali for ages. She's tall, slim, with the looks of a Leslie Caron, quite flat-chested but with legs that seem to go on forever. She's in her last year in 6th form doing A Levels and expecting to get a place at uni. If she does, it will be a serious loss to the band. Now, in her hound's-tooth mini skirt and black polo neck sweater, she could easily be mistaken for one of those serious, yet sexy, French students.

About halfway through the set, she and I duet on *I Got You Babe*, the difference being I take Cher's part and she takes Sonny's. It always gets a big laugh. As we sing, I give her a big smile, which she returns with warm, friendly eyes. I don't think she realises I fancy her; in fact, she usually seems quite nervous around me when we're not on stage. She takes her music seriously and doesn't join in the banter around the band when we're packing up, ready to go. If it wasn't for her brother asking her to play in the band, bribing her with the promise of a share of the hundred quid we might get, I seriously doubt she would have bothered. The "pop" songs and dance music we play aren't really her "thing", just a means to an end for some pocket money and the opportunity to practise her keyboard skills. Left to her own devices, she would much prefer to be playing something more edgy or experimental.

And every time I look at her, I fancy her even more.

Ali's brother Steve always stands to the far right of the stage, almost separating himself from the rest of us. Like his sister, he has a gift for music. Last year, he managed to get a place at an art school where he doesn't seem to produce much artwork but spends more time practising music. Since he first picked up a guitar when he was twelve and taught himself to play, he finds it easy to imitate any of the famous guitarists you hear on the radio or see on TV. Unlike the rest of the guys in the group who tend not to think about what they wear on stage – usually ending up in jeans and t-shirts – Steve likes to wear a black shirt and tight black jeans. It gives him a moody look, enhanced by his lack of engagement with the audience, whom he barely acknowledges, staring with heavy concentration at his guitar, his floppy black hair straying over his eyes. Given the rounds of applause and whistles of approval he receives after every solo – and there are a lot in the music we play – most of us would love this level of praise and approval. He, on the other hand, will look up with a half-smile, half-smirk. This doesn't deter the group of suburban girls dancing in front of him, attracted to his hint of danger and trouble, and hoping with teenage eagerness they might be the one he deigns to talk to during our thirty-minute break.

Keith is the complete opposite of Steve. He's the type people would call "big-boned", with more fat on his body than muscle and his chubby face and soon-to-be-thinning sandy hair. His main reason for being in the band is because his parents live in a big house with a detached garage and they let us use it to practise. He plays bass guitar, to be honest not very well, but what he lacks in musical talent he makes up for with huge enthusiasm for the band, arranging most of our gigs and sorting out bookings and travel and making sure we get together at least once a week to practise. On stage, he has a natural confidence, dancing around, smiling at the audience and getting them to join in and "make some noise!" And if his playing isn't quite up to scratch then either Steve or Ali will cover up any bum notes he might strike. It's impossible not to like him, and in a way, it's his enthusiasm and positive nature that keep us together. Plus, his parents are really chuffed we named the band after the family pet.

It's coming to the end of the evening and our two-hour set is just about over.

We finish with an encore of *Hi Ho Silver Lining;* it gets everyone on the floor for one more sweaty, sing-along dance before they drift back to finish their drinks and say their goodbyes.

There's a rhythm to the way we unwind and pack up. First, finish the last of our free drinks while Keith, me and Steve have a smoke. Dave starts packing up his drum kit and carts it off to the Land Rover, followed by Keith and his gear. I help Ali with her keyboard and load it into the Mini while Steve carries his guitar and amp. The whole process takes no more than thirty minutes, by which time we're in the car park saying goodbye.

'Don't forget Chorleywood next Saturday!' shouts Keith out of the window as Dave drives off.

I pick up one of the spare amps and head off towards my car. Contrary to what had been said earlier in the changing room, Pete's sister, Pete's gorgeous sister, wanders over and smiles.

'Hi, Marco, any chance of a lift?'

THREE

1966

The phone rings in my office. It's Brian, our boss the Creative Director.

'How are you and John getting on with that campaign for Horleys?'

John and I are the junior creative team at the agency – he's the art director and I'm the copywriter. 'It's looking good, Brian,' I say, trying to sound positive. 'Do you want to see what we've got so far?'

'Yes, please. Bring it round.'

Horleys is a national chain of garden centres. Their new marketing manager decided he wanted a London agency – probably hoping a successful campaign might get him another promotion. There isn't a huge budget, which is probably why John and I have been given the account to work on. The media people have planned a campaign based on local press and radio that will go out in the build-up to Easter. At least it allows us some big spaces and plenty of airtime.

John isn't back from lunch – I'm guessing he's still down the Barley Mow chatting up the new girl in the production department – so I grab the layouts and head up to Brian's office on the third floor. Sally, his secretary, strides out of his door wearing what she would call a modest mini skirt and what most normal people would call a pelmet.

'Hi, Marcus,' she purrs, looking at me from under long lashes. She is so unbelievably good-looking she makes me nervous. I'm never quite sure if she's flirting or teasing.

'Hi, Sal,' I manage, trying to sound as neutral as possible and resisting the urge to turn and watch her gorgeous arse sway down the corridor. Something her radar will have picked up, causing a satisfied smile to settle on her sultry lips.

Brian is leaning back in his chair, hands linked behind his head, his eyes shut, when I enter. I wait for him, not wanting to disturb his thoughts. (He might have been thinking about a new ad campaign, or maybe he was just imagining what sex would be like with Sally. Who knows?) I glance around the room, taking in the row of DADAs and Golden Lions on the shelf, the framed photos on the wall of Brian with other big names in the industry and the set of golf clubs in the corner. He must be about fifty-five and a founding partner in the agency – one of the creative "hot shops" that sprung up in the sixties. Famous for his beautifully crafted copy, his vow not to work on a cigarette account and not least for his thick crop of silver hair, he is something of a hero to me.

He opens his eyes and swivels round to face me. 'Hullo, Marcus. No John?'

'No,' I lie, 'he had to shoot out.'

'Okay, let's see what you've got.'

I put the layouts down one by one on his desk and wait for him to speak.

The idea we've come up with relies on distinctive illustrations rather than photos, coupled with amusing headlines, which I'm the first to admit are a bit punny but seem to work: "*Get fresh in the garden*", "*Natural Break*" and "*Spend this weekend in someone else's garden*", for example.

Brian looks up and smiles. 'So, why have you gone down this route?'

I pause for a few seconds. 'Well, we looked at what other centres are doing and it's all small pictures of plants and big prices. We want to make Horleys a destination for new gardening ideas rather than just another place to get your bedding plants and compost.'

I waited for him to absorb my rationale. 'Good. I like it. Have you done the radio yet?'

'No, I thought I'd wait to see how this went.' At least I was being honest.

'Okay. You'll have to be more direct on radio. Puns are great in print but don't work in a script. It'll give you the chance to talk more about product and price. That'll keep the client happy too. Bring me a couple of scripts tomorrow and then we'll go and see Derek.' Derek is the Account Director; he's okay for a "suit". Clients like him because he's good at entertaining, and we creatives like him because he's good at selling our work. He drives a Lotus Cortina, and rumour has it he's sleeping with Pam, his secretary.

I gather up the layouts and leave Brian's office feeling as if I've had a pat on the head from my old headmaster. In other words, quite chuffed.

When John gets back, I tell him what Brian had said and ask him how it had gone with the new girl. 'Waste of time and drinks.' He shrugged. 'She's got a bloody boyfriend.'

A couple of hours later, after I've knocked out a couple of scripts, the phone rings.

'Hey, Marco. Keith here.' Keith has just started work selling space for one of the new freesheets. Most people thought this was a crazy idea. We were all used to buying our newspapers, not having them shoved through our letterboxes without being asked. Where was the value? Where was the editorial content? As it turned out, most people didn't give a toss. They liked the local news, the free ads to sell their unwanted stuff and not having to buy the paper. Within three years, Keith would be managing director of the publisher of fifty freesheets and on his way to his first million when the company is sold. With the money he makes, he sets up a national magazine selling used cars which later becomes a successful website which spawns a major comparison website that is sold to a multi-national media company, and along the way he make himself several more million. But that will all be in the future.

'How would you like to spend your summer holiday in someplace called Cunit, in Spain?'

'Called what?'

'I know. Sounds hilarious, doesn't it?'

'What are you talking about, Keith?'

'I've got us a booking in a bar run by a couple of English guys. Turns out the brother of one of them heard us at the rugby club and put in a good word. Two weeks, free board and lodging and as much as you can drink.'

'When are you thinking about? Have you spoken to the others?'

'First two weeks in August. It's no problem for Steve and Ali, they're both students. I'm okay, so it's just you and Dave. Come on! It should be a laugh!' I had to admit it was tempting. I hadn't fixed any holiday, and Spain sounded more exotic than my parents' empty caravan in Wales.

'Yeah, sounds good. Count me in. I'll just need to check it out with work first.'

'Great!' says Keith. 'I'll tell Dave we need him to say yes, too. See you Saturday,' and with that, he hung up before I could say 'Bye.'

Before I leave for the day, I make my way back to Brian's office or, to be precise, Sally's cubbyhole next door.

'Hi, Marcus. Twice in one day.' She's applying fresh gloss to her perfect lips. 'To what do I owe the pleasure?' Again, I can't tell if she's flirting or teasing.

'I'd like to book some holiday. Do you have a form or something?'

'Mmm, going somewhere nice?' She delves in a drawer and brings out a sheet of paper. 'Fill this in and I'll give it to Brian.'

'Spain,' I manage to say. 'We've got a booking for the band.'

'Oooh, sounds lovely. Are you taking your girlfriend?'

This is about the longest conversation I've ever had with Sally. 'Er, no. I don't have a girlfriend, actually.'

'I find that hard to believe, Marcus, good-looking boy like you.'

She gives me a long, lingering, direct look until I can feel myself beginning to blush. 'Maybe you'd like to take me with you.'

Now I know she's teasing.

Two years later, after I'd left the agency, I reminded her of this conversation. 'I always thought you were a nice boy, Marcus,' she purred, pulling the sheet back and climbing on top of me. 'Now, are you going to stop talking and fuck me again?' Her voice suggested it was a rhetorical question that required no response except immediate input from myself.

FOUR

Here we are, loading the cars ready to leave for Spain. Dave's got most of the stuff – drums, amps, keyboard, guitars, speakers – in the back of the Land Rover. Alison has been allowed to borrow her mum's Mini on the understanding she only lets Steve co-drive. Her mother obviously doesn't trust Keith or myself with either her car or more probably her daughter. Little did she know that her son would spend most of the time drinking his way through large chunks of France, obliging either Keith or myself to share the driving with Alison, thus undermining her mother's concerns on both counts.

    We'd spent the previous afternoon at Keith's watching the World Cup Final on their new TV, bought especially for the occasion with the biggest screen available. To be honest, none of us were big football fans, but it was an exciting game and great to see England win, especially beating Germany. We all cheered as Bobby Moore lifted the trophy and laughed as Nobby Stiles danced around with his toothless grin. We could hear people cheering in the street outside and cars honking their horns.

Who could have believed we'd go winless for another fifty years or more?

We arrive in Newhaven in plenty of time to catch the ferry. Keith offers me a Rothmans and we study the maps, plotting the best route to the Spanish border and calculating how long it will take us to reach Cunit. We still can't help sniggering at the oddly suggestive name. We also can't find it on any of the maps we've brought along – we just know it's a village by the sea about 50 miles south of Barcelona. We guess we'll be able to find it when we get nearer Sitges. Our route will take us right down the N7, crossing over the border near la Jonquera. Doing a rough miles-per-hour calculation, we reckon it will take us about twenty-four hours if we don't stop too often, taking it in turns to drive every couple of hours.

We decide to stock up on the ferry with drinks and food for the journey. That way, we don't have to stop to eat or spend our foreign money.

Once on board, I find a seat and watch the harbour wall slide past the window, the coastline slowly shrinking behind us.

'Right, chaps,' says Keith, 'I suggest we all try and get some kip. Long way to go and all that.'

We laugh and pretend to shut our eyes, but we're too excited to think about sleep. Keith's wondering if we've got the right plugs for Spain, Dave's worrying about his mum he's left on her own, Steve's thinking about going to the bar, Alison's got her A level results to think about, and I'm musing on whether I might get into her knickers on this trip. I know, how shallow!

As it turns out, it takes us twenty-eight hours to get there, mainly because the Mini gets a puncture somewhere near

Limoges and then we get lost driving through Barcelona. Luckily, the Bar Estudio – our destination – is still open when we arrive outside the entrance at 3am. In fact, the place is going full swing. *River Deep, Mountain High* is blaring from the speakers, people are either dancing or crowding around the bar, some have spilled out into the night air, smoking, drinking, chatting, kissing.

This all looks very promising, I think to myself, making a mental note of the number of attractive young women within gazing distance.

A handsome man of about thirty walks out of the bar to greet us. Staggers out would be more accurate – he looks like he's had as much to drink as some of the other patrons. He smiles and introduces himself as James, one of the owners. He has that cultured, casual manner of someone who's been to a good school. 'But please call me Jim. Come in, come in and have a drink.' He puts a friendly arm around Dave, who flinches fractionally, not being used to such contact from a male he's never met before.

'Leave your stuff in the cars. We'll sort it out in the morning. Let me show you where you're sleeping.' We traipse in behind him, feeling somewhat out of place and totally sober amongst the crowd of happy, partying people.

It soon becomes clear that James didn't realise the band included a girl. We find two rooms above the bar with five single beds, which means someone is going to have to share with Alison. As much as I'd like to put my hand up straight away, she preempts my offer by stating she will share with her brother for one night only. We're all knackered anyway from the journey, so we agree to sort out a better sleeping plan the next day. Alison and Dave decide to crash out right away. Keith, Steve and myself decide it would be rude not to return to the bar for a beer or two. After all, we're on holiday, aren't we?

FIVE

I'm woken by a shaft of bright sunlight streaming through a crack in the window shutter, shining onto my pillow. When I move my head a couple of inches, it feels like I'm already sunbathing. I look at my watch on the bedside table: eleven-fifteen. I've slept for nearly seven hours. Looking around, I see Dave's bed is empty, while Keith is snoring gently. The room has the strong smell of body odour and human wind. I get out of bed a little unsteadily –last night's beers – pull on a pair of jeans and open the door.

'Morning, Marcus. Wondered when you'd surface.' Dave is sitting at a large wooden table with what looks like a giant sandwich in his hand. 'This bread is great, fresh from the baker next door, you should try some. There's coffee in the pot if you want one.'

'Yeh, thanks,' I mumble. 'I need a piss first.'

I explore the apartment. As well as the two rooms for the band, there are two more bedrooms on this floor, with a dining area in between. It turns out the other rooms are where the staff sleep: Martin, the barman, and Sue, who helps Jim with the cooking and cleaning. I find another door leading to a small kitchen and a bathroom, just big enough for a shower and toilet. The shower is one luxury we will come to love or loathe depending on whether the local water supply is on or off.

I rejoin Dave, still steadily munching.

'Did you get bitten last night?' He shows me his swollen ankles. 'Bloody mosquitos, I could hear them buzzing around all night. Every time the noise stopped, I knew I was going to get bitten. We'll have to find a way to get rid of them tonight.'

I give Dave a sympathetic shrug. 'Maybe they prefer your blood to mine, or maybe you need to drink more beer.'

I tear off a chunk of bread, cover it in butter and apricot jam and help myself to a cup of coffee, already feeling brighter. The bedroom door opens and Keith stumbles out. 'Jesus, what time is it?' He looks decidedly rough.

By midday, everyone's up and gathered around the table, discussing what to do first. Me and Steve are all for going to the beach for a swim. Keith, Ali and Dave feel we should get the gear unloaded and set up for a practice first, then go to the beach. They win.

We spend the next couple of hours unloading our stuff and getting set up on the small stage at the rear of the bar. The square space between the stage and the bar is the dancefloor. More than thirty people and you could say the atmosphere will be intimate. By now, we've learnt our playlist pretty well by heart, so the practice session is really more of a sound check. More importantly, it's a test of the bar's Spanish electrics to make sure our equipment doesn't overload the power supply.

Jim stands behind the bar nodding his approval. Apart from a couple of early customers, the place is empty. 'You guys sound great!' He pops the tops off a bunch of beers and stands them on the counter. 'Come and have a drink. You must be thirsty.' We leave the equipment and join him at the bar.

'So, what time do you want us to start tonight, Jim?' asks Keith.

He thinks for a moment. 'Let's see, most people spend the day at the beach, then they'll have a bit of a sleep, then they'll eat, then they'll begin to wander in here between nine and ten. How about you start at ten-thirty? If you play for an hour or so, you can have a break and I'll get Martin to play some records, before you start again. He fancies himself as a bit of a DJ. Would that suit you?' It sounds ideal. We finish our beers and everyone decides to head to the beach.

In front of the bar is an unmade roadway that turns into a dusty track to the beach. We have to stoop under a low bridge that carries the railway to Barcelona on a line that separates the village from the sea. The beach looks deserted, stretching out for miles in each direction. No buildings, no bars, no cars; not like a seafront at all, just sand and sea. It's as if the locals don't realise they've got all this on their doorstep. A couple of hundred yards to the north, I can see the canvas roofs of a campsite. About the same distance to the south, there appears to be a shed with a few people sitting under umbrellas.

'Come on, Keith, let's go and explore.' I'm pointing in the direction of the shed. He drops his towel on the beach, lights a cigarette and nods a "Yes." Alison and Dave are busy arranging themselves on the sand, Steve is heading in the direction of the sea for a swim as we saunter along, cooling our feet in the water.

'So, what do you make of it so far?' I ask.

'You mean the beach or the bar?'

'Both,' I reply.

Keith adjusts his sunglasses and flicks his cigarette into the sea. 'Well, if this was a beach in England, with weather like this, there'd be thousands here, so I guess the Spanish don't do summer holidays; or maybe they're all at work. Or maybe this isn't your typical holiday destination like Lloret or Torremolinos. Either way, it looks like we've got it all to ourselves, which is great!'

'And the Bar Estudio?'

'Should be a doddle. Jim seems a decent bloke too. All we have to do is turn up and play at night and have a good time during the day. Food, drink, bed all included, maybe a shag too!' Keith slaps me on the back. 'What's not to like?'

What we thought was a shed turns out to be a bar made of timber bleached by the sun. It stands on a slab of concrete with crates of empty bottles stacked up in the shade along one wall. A few people are sitting at tables, shielded from the sun by the umbrellas we could see from a distance, their faded fabric providing some relief from the heat.

'This looks more promising,' says Keith as we amble up to the counter.

A small tanned man of indeterminate age appears out of the shadowed interior. 'Two beers,' says Keith, holding up two fingers, assuming the man doesn't speak English but at least understands "beer". The man turns and delves into what looks like a giant picnic box full of ice and pulls out two bottles. He flips the tops off and places them neatly in front of us.

Keith fishes out a note from his shorts. The man smiles and hands him some change. The whole transaction has taken place in silence.

We grab our beers and find an unoccupied table. 'Well, that's the language problem sorted,' I say, as we clink bottles together.

By the time we get back to the others, Steve has had a swim and is lying on his back drying off in the sun. Dave is looking hot and bothered.

'It's a bit too hot for me,' he says, looking up and shielding his eyes as we approach. 'I'm going to have to find some shade soon or I'll burn.'

'Didn't you bring any suntan lotion with you?' asks Keith.

'Yes, I did, but I know I'll still burn. I've got that sort of skin.' He sounds rather forlorn, what with his mosquito bites as well.

'Tell you what, Dave,' I offer, 'we can drive into Sitges later and see if we can buy a beach umbrella and maybe some stuff for your bites. We'll probably all need some soon. How about that?'

Dave smiles ruefully. 'Thanks, Marcus, you're a pal.'

Alison is lying on her towel. She's wearing a pale blue bikini, a broad-brimmed straw hat and round-rimmed sunglasses. She continues to look like a French student, only this time *en vacances.* I've never seen her without clothes before. Correction, it's the first time I've seen her without either her school uniform or her stage outfit. She looks amazing.

I wonder if she's looking at me through her sunglasses as I stare at her through mine. The idle thoughts I had on the ferry about sleeping with her suddenly seem less like a fantasy and more like a possibility.

I nudge Steve on the ankle with my foot. 'Hey, Steve, what's the water like?' He doesn't say anything but lifts his arm and gives me a thumbs-up. I pull off my shirt and jeans and start running towards the sea, Keith a few yards behind. We both yell as we leap into the water, the warm Mediterranean closing in over our pale English skin.

After a couple of hours on the beach, we decide to head back to the village. Everyone's hungry and we need to eat before we perform tonight.

We crowd into the only restaurant we've seen so far, a short walk from the bar. The interior is empty except for an old lady dressed in black sitting in one corner. She looks at us without smiling. She's probably thinking, *Foreigners!* We sit down at one of the tables and chat away until a man emerges from another door. Thinking he might be a waiter, we attempt to ask for a menu. The man looks at us for a few moments then points to his watch and spreads his hands as if to say, *What time do you think this is? Too late for lunch, too early for dinner.* He shrugs then decides that five customers are better than no customers and brings us a menu. We pool our collective knowledge of the Spanish language and decide we can translate "chicken", "squid" and "chips", which we happily order, together with a round of beers.

We carry on drinking, smoking and talking. Before long, the man reappears, carrying plates piled high with fried chicken and squid rings and a huge basket of chips. We ask for more beers and tuck in. The food is delicious, like nothing any of us have ever tasted before, and soon disappears. Even Steve, who looks so skinny you'd think he never eats, smiles with pleasure, a dribble of hot juice sliding down his chin.

When the bill arrives, we can't believe the ludicrously small amount of *pesetas* it comes to, and we leave the man probably a far-too-generous tip. The restaurant is soon installed as our favourite place to eat, and Sergio, who is the owner and the waiter, becomes a friendly face, welcoming us with open arms and bringing us a continuous order of fried chicken. Meanwhile, the old lady in black hasn't smiled once.

While we've been at the beach, Jim has sorted out a sleeping arrangement for Alison. She's going to share a room with Sue, the student, which means that Dave can move in next door with Steve. Everyone's happy with this plan and the others drift off to get some rest while Dave and I take the Land Rover into Sitges, as promised.
It's nearly 9pm when we get back, just enough time to shower and pull on a clean pair of jeans and a loose shirt before heading downstairs to the bar.
The place looks surprisingly empty apart from half a dozen people drinking at the bar. Jim stands up from restocking the shelves and smiles, recognising the look of mild concern on my face.
'Don't worry, it's early yet. People like to eat late. There'll be a lot more here by the time you start. We'll be full by midnight once your band gets going, at least that's the general idea.' He laughs and slides a beer over the counter to me.
I spot Alison and Dave by the stage and wander over. They've already begun checking the equipment again, so I put down my beer to give them a hand.
'Anyone nervous?' I ask no one in particular. This is our first gig in what you might call a nightclub. We're used to playing in rugby clubs, village halls, marquees at weddings and birthdays, in front of an audience who we often know and who've heard us before and know what to expect.
'The only thing I'm nervous about, mate, is the power supply,' says Dave. 'Some of these sockets look decidedly dodgy. Let's hope no one gets electrocuted!' Alison bites

her lip and looks at me as if to say, *We will be all right, won't we?* It's true to say Alison always gets a bit nervous, even in England. She twiddles a strand of hair and hops a bit from foot to foot.

'Don't worry, Ali,' I say, 'if anyone's going to get a shock, it will be me from that mike.' She glances up at me and smiles.

True to his word, the bar is beginning to fill up. Martin has been playing a selection of soft rock over the PA system from tapes and LPs he brought with him.

Now, as we step onto the stage, I estimate there are about fifty people crowded around the bar, although none, so far, on the dancefloor.

Martin taps the microphone to get some attention then announces, 'Ladies and gentlemen, boys and girls, please welcome for the first time at the Bar Estudio, Alexander's Relations!' He claps loudly and on this cue we break into *Green Onions*.

After a couple of numbers, people stop talking and start listening, and before long, there's enough of a crowd on the dancefloor to create a good atmosphere. Looking down from the stage, I see a bunch of twenty-somethings not paying us much attention but clapping after each number and having a good time. *This all seems to be going very well*, I think to myself, smiling at a very attractive blonde who returns a shy smile. *Another two weeks of this could be right up my street.*

We take a break and have a huddle by the stage to iron out any problems, of which there seem to be very few. Our main concern is moving about on the small stage and tripping over a cable. We decide to ask Jim in the morning for some gaffer tape to fix the cables to the floor and some old carpet to cover them up. Keith, our "leader", is happy with our first set and wanders off to have a word with Jim.

I stroll across the dancefloor and head for the door to get some fresh air, nodding at a few smiles directed towards me but mainly ignored by the patrons who have returned to their drinks at the bar.

Leaning against the wall, lighting a Gitanes, I notice the blonde moving towards me, glass in hand.

'Hi,' she says, again that shy smile.

'Hullo,' say I, exhaling smoke. 'Are you having a good time?'

'Yes. My friends and I are really enjoying your music. Where are you from?'

Her English is good but with an accent that sounds to me, not French, but maybe Dutch or German.

'Near London, how about you?' I give her a full-on smile and offer her a cigarette, which she accepts and takes a light off mine.

'I'm from Switzerland, from Zurich. Do you know it?' So, my German guess wasn't too far off the mark.

'Well, I've heard of it but never been there. How did you find this place?' I nod my head towards the bar.

'We're on holiday. My parents have a villa not far from here. We come to Spain often. But this is the first time we hear music in the bar. Your band is very good.' She smiles again, showing me a perfect set of white teeth. She really is very pretty and by the look of her tan has spent some time here already.

'Well, thank you very much. Always good to hear a satisfied customer.' I lean towards her. 'So, what's your name, girl from Zurich?'

'Ingrid.' She smiles, stubbing out the cigarette with a twist of her sandal. 'What's yours?'

'Marcus, but you can call me Marco. Most people do.'

'Okay. Hi, Marco.' She looks straight at me. 'Maybe see you on the beach tomorrow?' Her eyes say *I want to see you* as she turns and heads back to her friends at the bar. I admire the sway of her hips and take a few moments, breathing in the warm air, listening to the chatter from the bar and looking up at the dark sky scattered with stars.

Fuck me, I think, *this is definitely turning out better than expected!*

Our second set gets under way. By now, there's a large crowd of people in the bar and more bodies on the dancefloor. The cheap beer and plentiful rum 'n' coke help everyone get in party mood. Inhibitions are being cast aside along with various items of clothing – soon the dancefloor is looking more like a beach party than a nightclub. Up on stage, we're dripping in the unconditioned air but loving it. People are clapping and shouting for encores – I think we've played *Hi Ho Silver* three times already – even Steve is smiling, and Alison has finally looked up from her keyboard and is waving at the audience. By the time we've struck our final chords and Dave has given one last beat on the drums, we're soaked in sweat and grinning at each other like we've just won *Thank Your Lucky Stars*.

Jim is heading towards us, weaving his way through the slowly dispersing dancers, carrying a tray of beers, a big smile on his face.

'That was great, guys!' he says, putting down the tray and handing out bottles. 'You really made a big impression. Once the word gets around, we'll have even more people in here. Well done!' He slaps Keith on the back and gives Alison a hug. 'Just ask Martin at the bar when you want more drinks.'

He wanders off to talk to one of his regulars. What we really want is fresh air and a chance to sit down, so we head outside and find ourselves a table, acknowledging a flurry of congratulations on the way. Keith looks over at me, cigarette in one hand, beer in the other, feet on the table. 'So, what do you think, mate? Glad you came?'

'You bet I am.' I smile back. 'Absolutely fucking great.'

We soon get into a routine.

Wake up around 10am, breakfast on fresh bread and jam – although Sue has started cooking us fried eggs, which we devour with pleasure – coffee, then check our gear from the night before. Down to the beach around noon for a sunbathe and swim.

Dave has found a folding chair and settles in the shade under the umbrella reading a paper, Alison lies on her towel and is stuck into a book, Keith and I swim and stroll to the beach bar for beers, Steve has taken to wandering off by himself towards the campsite. I'm beginning to think he's found a drinking buddy or maybe someone to smoke dope with. Either way, by the time we head off the beach around 4pm, he's looking slightly out of it.

By late afternoon, we're at Sergio's, eating fried chicken and drinking cold beers. He seems to have got used to our odd eating times and is happy to have some regular customers. Even the old lady has nodded and smiled.

Then it's time for a kip for a couple of hours before showering and getting down to the bar for a drink or two before we're back on stage again.

The days and nights pass by and everyone is happy. We seem to have found ourselves on an island of hedonism, separated from the outside world, where a cultured group of young, attractive Europeans have gathered together to share in the golden summer of 1966. Or, more likely, it's the result of Jim's network of contacts made from art school in London and Berlin.

In case you were wondering about Ingrid, the smiling girl from Zurich, I do meet her on the beach. Turns out she's here with her sister and a couple of friends from school. Yes, they're all about seventeen. At the beach, they look much younger than they did in the bar – friendly, open, fresh faces without make-up – but with very desirable bodies. Ingrid is keen to show me her parents' villa. So, one afternoon, we wander off and walk a mile or so inland. Surprise, surprise, her folks are out for the day. Somehow we end up in the pool, without any clothes, and then we're drying on the terrace; kissing, touching, stroking, and pretty soon we're having the most delightful fuck. As we lie next to each other in that dreamy after-sex state, smoking, Ingrid leans over, kisses me and says, 'I'm sorry, Marco. I won't see you again.'

I raise a hand to shield my eyes. 'Why? What happened?'

'Nothing. It's just that we're going home tomorrow.'

I can't help wondering if I've just become a notch on Ingrid's bedpost rather than the other way around.

As it happens, by the start of our second week in Cunit, I've struck up a very friendly relationship with Sue, the student helper. She's the first to admit she's *jolie laide* (she's studying French), but she owns an amazing body with an enthusiastic appetite for sex and a willingness to try anything, at least once. We begin to refer to our "*cinq à sept*" – the hours we should be spending sleeping but spend fucking instead.

Despite my earlier shallow intentions, I never did get to make a move on Alison. Before long, she had acquired a fan club of three young French guys who followed her everywhere, entranced by her musical prowess and "look, don't touch" body. She told me years later she felt like she was living in an existential novel.

By the time it came to pack up our gear and say goodbye to the Bar Estudio, we all agreed we'd had the best time ever. Tanned, exhausted, musically improved, friendships made – and all without spending much of our dosh, thanks to Jim's hospitality. He's made us a very generous offer to come back next year. We say "yes", of course, because we're polite young people, but the reality is that next year is way too far ahead.

SIX

1996

You may be wondering how I can afford to live in an affluent area like Holland Park.

I began renting my apartment in the early seventies. A top-floor flat up three flights of stairs, with big windows and a nice view over the gardens in the square below. It was part of a large portfolio of property in the area owned by the church that still retained an old-fashioned commitment to affordable rents. It was a stroke of luck I found the flat in the first place – one of those rare collisions of fate when I got chatting to the outgoing tenant at a party. She happened to mention, as we shared a smoke lying in her bed later that evening and I'd been very complimentary about her good taste in decorating, that she was moving to Bristol. I'd been slightly put off by her small dog trying to lick my arse while I was on top of its mistress – it wasn't so much the licking, more the thought the dog wanted to make it a threesome. Anyway, she told me she'd have to give up the flat and asked if I knew anyone who might be interested.

It was too good an opportunity to miss. I applied for the lease the very next day, helped by a glowing endorsement from the aforementioned tenant.

Built in the 1800s, most of the former merchants' houses had been divided into flats many years before. And despite its proximity to the busy Bayswater Avenue, the Square retained a quiet charm, its gated garden providing a privileged haven for those residents fortunate enough to have acquired a key. The large ground-floor apartment was occupied by an ageing actor and his wife, plus two King Charles Spaniels. He had been one of the angry young men of British cinema in the early sixties who then went on to star in a hugely popular series of gritty police dramas on TV. She had been a dancer at the London Palladium. Although the acting work had largely dried up, apart from a couple of television commercials, his was a well-recognised face and so he hardly left the apartment. After we'd met a few times in the hallway and he realised I wasn't another autograph hunter, we got on really well. They were lucky enough to own the rear garden and I would spend time with him helping to tidy the borders and prune the shrubs, under his strict instructions. Fanny, his wife, would bring out a tray of tea and biscuits, and he and I would sit under the shade of the magnolia tree and share, for him, a forbidden cigarette while he entertained me with bitchy gossip about his fellow actors. They were a truly lovely couple.

The apartment suited my lifestyle perfectly. Five minutes' walk to the Tube, fifteen minutes on the Central Line to my office in Bond Street. By now, I was a senior copywriter at a multinational agency and beginning to acquire a reputation within the industry, picking up the odd award, and getting well paid. I liked to move jobs every couple of years or so; not unusual in the advertising business. I'd been headhunted a few times for positions with more responsibility, but I liked the writing and working as a team with an art director, without the distraction of the politics of management.

Girlfriends came and went. My longest relationship was with Monique, a gorgeous French girl I met at the Royal Academy's Summer Exhibition. I couldn't help noticing the glossy black hair, great legs and leopard print coat. She stood for a long while in front of an abstract painting and I couldn't resist going over to her and asking, 'So what do you think the artist is trying to say?' I know, corny, but true.

She continued looking for a moment or two before turning to me. 'I think he's saying, "My mind is full of ideas, but I don't know how to express them." Maybe that's why it's called Untitled 31.' I laughed; it was one of those moments of mutual instant attraction.

'Coffee?'

She smiled. 'Why not?'

She told me she worked in the London office of a French bank, something to do with the legal side. The combination of brains, looks and her French accent was extremely potent.

She was one of the few people, apart from my parents, who called me Marcus, although with her accent it became "Marr-cusse." It never failed to excite me, whether we were having a laugh or an argument or making love.

She never actually moved in with me in Norland Square; her office in Docklands made it an awkward journey, but she'd stay weekends, preferring the sophistication of West London to the rougher edges out east. We even managed a couple of holidays together, long weekends in Rome and Madrid, but she was an ambitious young woman, and when her bank offered her a position in Geneva it was an offer she couldn't refuse. We had a long, tearful goodbye with promises to stay in touch, but eventually our letters and phone calls became less and less frequent. A few years later, she wrote to say she was getting married to a Swiss lawyer named Eric. She sent this news on a postcard with an abstract painting on the front. The memory made me smile even as I sighed.

It was late one afternoon in the office when my mobile rang. I'd been an early adopter of the new phone technology in the nineties. I admit it was kind of a status symbol, a trait us "shallow" advertising types shared with estate agents.

The sound interrupted me from the thought process of putting together some words for a headline – although anyone looking through the door might have wondered if I was taking a nap. Sometimes, they would have been right.

I quickly scribbled down a couple of words before picking up the phone. 'Hullo, Marcus speaking.'

'Hi, Marcus. It's me, Nigel, at Angel.'

Nigel was a sound engineer at Angel, the recording studio we used for TV soundtracks and radio commercials.

'Hi, Nige, how's it going?' I imagined he was phoning about the mix for the soundtrack of a new TV ad I'd just written for our German car client.

'Yeah, it's going great, should have something for you to listen to by tomorrow. Actually, it was something else I'm calling about.'

'Sounds intriguing. What have you got?'

'You remember that music track of yours we were playing about with a while back? Well, someone was in here today, heard it and really liked it.'

When Alexander's Relations finally packed up in 1970, basically because we all had busy jobs and couldn't find the time or be bothered to practise, I kept up my interest in music. I went to a lot of pub gigs around town listening to whoever was new on the scene. I could kid myself I was looking for new talent or trying to capture the *zeitgeist*, but actually I just liked going to the pub, having a couple of pints, listening to the band and maybe chatting up a girl; usually, I must admit, without much success.

Some nights back at my flat I would play around with my tape machine, recording snatches of songs or putting down a melody I liked. It became a hobby, something I enjoyed doing, like someone taking up painting or writing a book.

Most of this stuff never saw the light of day, but occasionally, if we had some time left over after a recording session at the studio, I would ask the engineer to put some polish on a couple of the tapes I thought might have some merit. Maybe worth sending to a record company or turning into a jingle.

It would not be an exaggeration when I say that Nigel's phone call changed my life.

When I went to see him the next day, he started by playing back the music track I'd left with him.

'Remember this?'

'Yeah, of course. That must have been two years ago, at least. So, what happened?'

'I had a guy in here yesterday working on some ideas for a new campaign. He asked if I had any thoughts for a jingle to go with the visuals. He was looking for a "boy meets girl, boy loses girl, boy finds girl" scenario, that type of thing. That's when I thought of your demo.'

'Wow!' I said. 'What happened?'

'He loved it! Took a copy back to the agency to play to his team, said it was perfect. You better get yourself an agent!'

It turned out the creative guy was working on a campaign for one of the big Scandinavian phone companies. They were launching a new mobile and wanted to reach a younger market, one that would see the phone as a social accessory rather than a business tool.

I followed Nigel's advice and found myself an agent who could negotiate with the phone company. They agreed on an initial payment for the track plus a royalty for every time the commercial was aired. After a test market in New Zealand, it was decided the campaign was successful enough to be rolled out around the English-speaking world. And for the next few years, the money kept rolling in; I mean, I made thousands!

As all this was happening, the property market in London was booming. The people who looked after the church's assets in Norland Square could see there was more money to be made from selling property than collecting low rents. When the letter dropped through my door offering my flat for sale, it was too good an opportunity to miss. We haggled a bit, they accepted my offer, I handed over the money and here I am: the owner of a lovely property in a desirable part of town, probably worth five times what I paid for it.

To begin with, I thought I would give up work, maybe make some new jingles or try my hand at a novel, but I liked my job at the agency and I knew I'd get bored if I didn't have the buzz of contact with other people. I'm a bit odd like that – I like being with my mates at work, but I'm happy with my own company at home. Maybe that's why I've never settled down with anyone. I like to live in the world on my own terms, make decisions that suit me.

So, I thought I'd just let the extra cash accumulate in the bank, like a golden nest egg, and kind of forget about it until something really important happened, sometime in the future.

SEVEN

1987 – ALISON

I wake up with a splitting headache. I turn my head slowly to the left to look at the clock – 8am. Jesus! I've only been in bed four hours. Moving my head to the right, I see Keith, fast asleep, snoring softly. I watch his chest rising and falling. The air in the room has the familiar smell of a heavy night; stale alcohol mixed with perfume and smoke. I lie back, forcing myself to keep my eyes open, trying to assemble the events of the night before.

My 40th birthday party.

It had all begun so well. Keith had planned everything with military precision; he's good at that sort of thing. The guests, the catering, the drinks, the marquee, the DJ, the parking. And the reunion of the band. I was happy to let him get on with it. If it had been left to me, I would have probably invited a few friends for dinner, but Keith said it was a special occasion and we should *celebrate.* He would never admit that what he really wanted to do was show off to his wealthy new friends that he used to be in a band.

Marcus and Dave arrived yesterday. My brother, Steve, is already here, much against Keith's wishes. But I'm his only family, and after his latest brush with the law, I can keep an eye on him, feed him too.

The idea was to have a rehearsal in the marquee, put together a set of numbers that we could turn into sixty minutes of live entertainment. It soon became apparent we would need more than an afternoon's rehearsal. It took ages to set up the equipment, tune the instruments, test the mikes. For five people who had stood on stages and played for hundreds of people, we seemed nervous of each other, almost embarrassed. It wasn't long before Keith had begun pacing up and down, rubbing his head in frustration.

'Come on, guys, we should all know this one. We've played it hundreds of times. Let's go again.' We waited for Dave to count us in before attempting another go at *Satisfaction*. After a few bars, Keith held up his hand, waving for us to stop.

'Jesus Christ, Steve, you're way behind. Are you really with us or are you on something?'

Steve had looked at Keith as if to say, *I know you're married to my sister and I'm living under your roof, but get off my back or I'm walking*. But didn't. Instead, he just smiled at Keith, which made him even angrier. Not for the first time in the band's history, Marcus, the peacemaker, stepped in.

'Okay, let's all calm down. Keith, mate, why don't you fetch us a few beers? I think we could all do with a drink. And, Steve, go and find something warmer to put on. You look freezing. No wonder you're a bit behind, your fingers must be bloody numb!'

It was true that Steve had taken to wearing a flimsy, floppy shirt in the style of Adam Ant. It might have looked fashionable in a photo but had no merit on an unseasonably cool day in June.

By the time we'd sunk a couple of beers and Steve had returned in a totally unfashionable jumper (one of Keith's golf sweaters, but he never noticed), we had relaxed enough to rediscover our rhythm. Two hours later, we were nodding and smiling at each other, confident that we could perform again without looking like idiots.

Easing myself slowly from the bed, I head for the bathroom to fetch a drink of water and a couple of paracetamol. Looking back at me from the mirror is not what some people are kind enough to say is the still-youthful face of a forty-year-old, but a crumpled version with swollen, bloodshot eyes. Have I been crying? I concentrate to hear if there's any sound downstairs, but the house stays silent, too early for anyone to be moving about. I swallow the pills and decide to head back to bed.

By 10pm, the party had begun to warm up. Why is it called a party? Parties are for children, ice cream and jelly and games, not for adults. This was very much a *function*. It may have been my birthday, but that was just an excuse. What Keith really wanted was to show off *his* house in this leafy former village at the end of the Metropolitan line; in what used to be called the stockbroker belt.

It was sweet of him to invite some of my pals from Oxford; he'd even tracked down a couple of old school friends. He must have spent ages looking for them.

Apart from Steve and my kids, Jake and Sophie, there was no other family. Mum and Dad were both gone and I was never one for keeping in touch with relations. The majority of guests, by far, were people Keith knew. Friends from the golf club, a few from his office, and clients. Lots of clients. His magazine business, his publishing *empire*, as he likes to call it after a few glasses of his favourite burgundy, relied on these clients, people with money to spend on advertising.

Guests flowed from the house to the garden to the marquee. Waiters circulated with trays of fizz and wine; buckets full of ice dotted around the garden held dozens of bottles of beer. It was Keith's idea to offer canapes; sausages wrapped in bacon, fish fingers, miniature beef burgers – "proper food", he called it – to soak up the drinks before the main meal of the evening: a hog roast carved by a chef and served with salads and new potatoes.

Everyone looked like they were having a great time, and after the first hour, people had stopped wishing me "Happy Birthday" and were getting on with enjoying themselves.

Around 10pm, Keith got hold of the mike from the DJ and announced that the band would be on in fifteen minutes. The five of us made our way to the stage and began to get ready. I felt my stomach tighten with nerves, a familiar sensation from the past.

Keith's voice amplified through the speakers: 'Ladies and gentlemen, boys and girls, lovely guests, tonight, we are celebrating a special birthday of my darling wife, Ali.' He waved his arm in my direction and clapped his hands. A polite cheer rose from the crowd and I gave a rather embarrassed wave in thanks. I was pretty sure Keith had told a lot of people he'd been in a band, but I don't think he'd told many people I'd been in it too, so I must have looked a bit of a curiosity.

'I thought,' Keith continued, 'it would be great fun if we got back together again on this special occasion for a one-night-only reunion. So, please, put your hands together for Alexander's Relations!' There was a ripple of applause as

Dave counted us in and we started to play. By the time we'd finished the first three numbers, I sensed everyone was beginning to relax, both the band and the audience. Marcus's voice sounded good and the marquee was filling with people dancing. Looking up, I could see Jake and Sophie at the back of the tent with the few friends Keith had allowed them to invite, pointing and laughing. To a bunch of fourteen-year-olds, I imagined it was probably more embarrassing than amusing to see adults – especially your parents – playing music from the sixties, and nothing their teenage tastes might have recognised.

We carried on playing, serving up more of the old favourites. Keith was beaming with delight, prancing up and down the stage like a middle-aged Mick Jagger, enjoying every moment, acknowledging the approving glances of his clients in the audience. He was in his element. And then it happened – Steve fell off the stage.

I couldn't tell whether he was drunk or high or just tripped, but he managed to play a crashing chord as he fell to the ground. Keith looked on in horror but instead of a concerned "Oh my God," a loud, angry "Oh, for fuck's sake, Steve!" came out of the mike clenched in his hand. Steve, bless him, managed a weak smile as he lay in a crumpled heap, but it was soon clear he had damaged his wrist in the process of falling and could take no further part in our performance. Keith looked around at the rest of us in the hope that we could carry on, but without our lead guitarist, we knew it wouldn't work. (Much later, I realised I could have played most of Steve's leads on my keyboard, but that option hadn't occurred to Keith.)

'Sorry, folks, it looks like we're down a man, so I guess we'll have to call it a night.' He was trying to keep it light-hearted, but I knew from the clench of his jaw he was fuming. Keith's "winding" motion to the DJ was his signal to get some music playing asap – he didn't want his party (my party?) to fizzle out. In truth, the guests didn't seem to be bothered by the lack of live music. They continued to take advantage of the hot and cold buffet and the free booze, not allowing Keith's disappointment to get in the way of a good time.

By 1am, the marquee was full of fairly drunk people swaying and weaving to the slower tunes played by the DJ. Small groups sat around in chairs or on the floor, smoking and chatting, while a few couples leant against walls, arms draped around each other. At one point, I saw Marcus, champagne bottle in one hand and a nubile young woman in the other, heading in the direction of the garden. Typical Marcus, I thought, so predictable. I looked around for Keith, but he was holding court with a group of his golfing buddies, looking as if they were sharing a joke. I had no desire to join them. God knows where Dave was, probably in bed already.

I wandered into the kitchen and poured myself a glass of fizz; it was my party, after all.

A while later, catching up with one of my old school friends thoughtfully invited by Keith, I became aware of a heated discussion going on by the front door. I could make out Keith's voice but couldn't identify the other.

'He's old enough to be her bloody father!' shouted the unknown voice. 'I've a good mind to call the police!'

'Come on, Guy, calm down. I don't think anyone actually forced her to go into the shed with him.' It was obvious from the placating tone of Keith's voice that Guy was one of his clients. 'How old is she anyway?'

'That's not the point!' blazed Guy. 'How would you like it if you found your daughter being shagged by some third-rate pop singer?' Lucy, the girl all the fuss was about, sat on the stairs, a man's jacket around her shoulders, one hand covering her eyes as if not wishing to witness her father's embarrassing outburst. Next to her stood Marcus, in shirtsleeves, nursing a bloody nose.

'Come on, Lucille, we're leaving, now! And don't think you've heard the last of this,' he added, turning to Keith.

The errant young woman handed the jacket back to Marcus and tiptoed up to kiss him on the cheek before her father grabbed her by the arm and dragged her through the door. Keith, meanwhile, looked like he wanted to add his own punch to Marcus's nose.

It later transpired that Guy, wishing to leave the party, had wandered around for half an hour looking for his daughter before continuing his search in the garden. Hearing noises from the shed, he'd barged in to find her enthusiastically astride Marcus. It was moments later that his fist connected with Marcus's face.

As I looked at Marcus, who seemed genuinely bemused by the whole episode, I couldn't help feeling that "third-rate pop singer" would have hurt him more than a bloody nose.

'Actually,' said Marcus to no one in particular, leaning against the bannister and exhaling smoke from a freshly lit cigarette, 'if we're going to be completely accurate about the whole thing, it was *she* who was shagging *me*.'

EIGHT

My head is still throbbing. As I wait for the paracetamol to kick in, I begin to think about Marcus. Oh, Marcus, I had such a crush on you! Why did you ignore me all those years ago? I'll admit I was painfully shy and did nothing to give you any clue as to how I felt. You used to smile at me when we sang together, but it was the kind of smile you'd give a sister, not a meaningful exchange of glances. Even when you helped me load the car or bought me a drink it felt like I was just Steve's kid sister. It didn't help that you seemed to be a magnet for the prettiest girls at the gigs we played at. What chance did I have; a skinny eighteen-year-old with glasses, against such confident competition?

If I'm honest, I wasn't that disappointed when the band broke up. I was at uni by then and didn't have the time or desire to go back and play boring pop songs to another drunken rugby crowd. My music scholarship was steering me in loftier directions, and I had ambitions to join a serious orchestra. It didn't quite turn out like that, but I did enjoy several years as a sought-after session musician before Keith came back into my life.

And now? Here we are, almost twenty years down the track; Marcus is still a very attractive man and I'm still married to Keith.

Right on cue, my husband begins to wake up. A few yawns and stretches and he's sitting up and reaching for his watch and a glass of water.

Instead of 'Morning, birthday girl' or 'Wow! what a night,' his first words are 'That fucking brother of yours and that fucking Marcus too! What a total shambles! God knows what it's cost me. That's the last time we get the band together.'

I have to hold myself back from reminding him it was his idea in the first place.

'Don't get angry, K. I don't think Steve meant to fall off the stage, and from what I could see, that girl with Marcus knew exactly what she was doing. I'm sure everyone had a lovely time. Besides, you can't have a birthday party without a few dramatic moments. That's what people remember!'

I decide it's time to get up to see what's happening in the rest of the house. 'I'm going to get breakfast started. Shall I bring you some tea?'

'Thanks, Ali, that would be nice. Sorry about the rant. Did you have a good time?' I give him a smile and a thumbs-up.

Downstairs is a mess. The caterers aren't due until eleven and every surface is littered with dirty plates and empty glasses apart from one corner of the kitchen table, where Dave and Marcus are eating cornflakes. I run a hand along Marcus's shoulder on my way to the fridge.

'Morning, naughty boy, how's the nose?'

He gives me a rueful grin. 'A bit sore but no major damage.'

I pour myself some juice. 'Well, I hope she was worth it, although I think you'll have to apologise to Keith later.'

'Is he mad?'

'Just a tad. Says it's probably going to cost him a fortune in lost business.' For a moment, Marcus looks anxious. 'Don't worry,' I say, 'only teasing, he'll get over it.'

'Did I miss something?' says Dave, looking around for somewhere to put his empty bowl.

'Just our Casanova here, breaking another girl's heart.'

'Hardly,' says Marcus. 'Probably have forgotten me by tomorrow.'

I busy myself clearing enough space to get breakfast going.

'If you want bacon and eggs, you'll have to give me a hand. I'm still pretty hungover.'

'Of course,' says Dave, never one to turn down a good meal. 'Here, I made some coffee.' He passes me a mug and pulls back a chair. 'Sit down, drink this. Marcus and I will get started, won't we?' He nudges Marcus, who seems on the point of falling asleep.

Good old Dave, always willing to give a hand. I've never really seen him with a girlfriend – maybe he's just too set in his ways.

I sit and stir sugar into my coffee – something I wouldn't normally do, but my headache craves sweetness – and supervise the two men as they navigate the kitchen. It's quite soothing to watch them working as a team; Dave is adept at cooking the eggs and bacon, he's even found mushrooms and tomatoes, while Marcus is busy on coffee and toast duty.

A face appears around the door. It's Sophie, looking rather sleepy and wondering if there's anything to eat.

'Good morning, my darling, what time did you go to bed?'

Sophie yawns and tries to think. 'Dunno, it must have been late, it was getting light. I just crashed.'

She wanders over to the table and makes a grab for the toast that Marcus has just made. 'Get off!' he says, giving her hand a tap with the butter knife. She pretends to sulk until he relents and hands over a slice.

Suddenly I remember Keith's tea. 'Sophie, love, put the kettle on and make your father a cup of tea and take it up to him. It'll put you in his good books and maybe you can talk to him about that French trip you want to go on.' Dutifully, she fills the kettle and leans against the worktop munching her toast.

'By the way,' I say, 'has anyone seen Steve this morning?'

Dave and Marcus exchange glances, as if they'd rather not say. 'Well,' says Dave, 'after the stage incident, I helped him find a bandage for his wrist. It was looking quite swollen, but I don't think it was broken. I asked him if he thought he should get it looked at, but he didn't seem too bothered.'

'And,' I say, 'was he high or drunk, or what?'

'He didn't seem drunk to me, more, like, happy, so I guess he was high, although I'm no expert,' says Dave.

'So, you haven't seen him since?'

Dave looks across at Marcus, waiting for him to say something.

'What is it?' My voice begins to convey my concern.

'Look, Ali, don't get too worried, but Dave told me he saw Steve driving off last night – in your car.'

Oh fuck! I think, *that's all I need. Keith's going to go ballistic.* 'Tell me you're joking!' Now I'm really beginning to panic.

'Sorry, Ali, it's true. I checked this morning to see if he's back but your car's not outside.'

I start to wonder how I'm going to put the words together to tell Keith. To tell him his birthday present to me, the BMW convertible, has gone and, even worse, that my brother took it.

Dave starts to serve up the breakfast and passes me a plate. I look at the food, but my appetite has gone. Picking up a rasher of bacon, I get up from the table.

'I'm going to have a bath,' I announce. Anything to delay explaining the situation to K.

I step in and slowly unfold beneath the water. I shut my eyes and feel my headache begin to ease as I relax in the warmth of the perfumed bath. My thoughts drift away from last night's party and the problem of Steve and the missing car. My mind wanders back to a time years ago, before I got married.

I can see myself in a pub having an evening drink with Jess, a girlfriend. We're in The True Lovers' Knot – the locals call it the TLK – and I've gone back to my parents for the weekend. I'd just been dumped by a boy, I think his name was Alan, and I'm pouring out my heart to Jess. Not that I'm heartbroken, just that I haven't had much success with the men in my life. Jess does her best to cheer me up and we sympathise with each other over our rotten choices.

Next thing I remember I'm standing at the bar ordering more drinks when a loud voice behind me exclaims, 'Hey, Ali, fancy seeing you in here!'

I turn around to see Keith, empty glass in hand, big smile on his face. 'Gosh, I haven't seen you for ages! How the hell are you?'

I smile back. 'Hi, Keith, I'm fine, thanks. Just back for the weekend.' The barman slides my drinks across the counter and I turn to pay.

'Let me get those,' says Keith, waving some cash.

'No, really, you don't have to,' I say, pushing his arm away.

'But I insist, really.' He grins. He pushes a note towards the barman. 'I'm getting a round in anyway,' and he nods towards a group of guys sitting by the window.

'Well, thank you. That's very kind. I'll tell Jess you bought the drinks.'

'My pleasure,' he adds. 'It's really good to see you, and looking great too!' I thank him again and head back to Jess.

'Who was that?' she asks immediately. 'He seemed very friendly.'

I explain to her that Keith is someone I used to play in the band with before I went to uni. 'I guess he must still live around here.'

She looks over in his direction. 'Mmm, quite nice-looking but a bit on the suburban side.' We share a secret giggle and clink glasses. 'Here's to men,' says Jess, 'sod them all!'

Next morning, after a late breakfast, Mum comes up to my room.

'Alison, dear, there's a young man at the door, wants to see you. I think it's Keith.'

'Keith? What does he want?'

'He didn't say, just wanted to know if you were here. He was very polite.'

I glance in the mirror, run a hand through my hair then head downstairs.

'Keith, hi. What on earth are you doing here?' I give him a puzzled smile.

'Hi, Ali, again.' He doesn't look so confident this time. 'I guessed you might be staying with your parents so I thought I'd pop by and say hullo. Wondered if you might like to go somewhere for lunch.'

I hesitate, stalling, trying to think of an easy way to say no.

'Well, that's very kind, Keith, but I was going to have lunch with my mum and dad.' I was just about to add 'maybe another time' when my mother, hovering in the hallway, chimes in.

'That's all right, Alison, you go. I'm sure you'd rather go out than stay here with your dad and me.'

'But, Mum... I wanted...' I can see she wants me to go. She's looking as if she's already sized up Keith as suitable husband material.

'Great!' says Keith, smiling and looking pleased with himself. He's actually rubbing his hands! 'I'll be back in an hour,' he says over his shoulder as he heads off down the drive.

I turn towards my mother. 'Thanks a million, Mum. I really didn't want to go.'

'Don't be so silly, darling. I'm sure you'll have a lovely time.'

As it happened, and much to my surprise, I did enjoy myself. Keith turned up in sixty minutes, precisely, in his sports car and whisked me off to a restaurant in Marlow, right by the river. He told me all about the newspaper business he was in, how it was growing rapidly and how he wanted to start a magazine. He was very attentive, very confident, and wanted to know all about my life after university.

He was very complimentary about my music, saying I was probably the most talented in our band, and wanted to hear all about my experiences as a recording "artiste", as he called me.

The food, the wine, the thick linen tablecloth and napkins, the crystal glasses, even the sun on the river reflecting on the pale blue ceiling, it was all just perfect, and I began to realise I was feeling very relaxed in Keith's company. Not to say he was what you would call dashingly handsome. When we'd been in the band, I hadn't really looked at him. He was just Keith on bass guitar and not very good on it, either, as I remember. Now, years later, I saw across the table a fairly average-looking man with a friendly face, wearing a sports jacket and tie – looking, as Jess would say, rather "suburban".

The meal over, we sat outside drinking coffee, watching the river boats go by.

'I'm so glad you decided to come,' he said, refilling my cup. 'To be honest, I was feeling a bit nervous, but it was such a lovely surprise to see you in the pub, I felt I must see you again.'

I was trying to think how to reply when a waiter arrived with the bill, which Keith duly paid with an impressive wad of notes.

And here I am, I think to myself, the water in the bath beginning to cool. Married with two kids, lovely children that they are. And Keith – successful, wealthy, sometimes grumpy – but still like a dog with a wagging tail, eager to please me. He's kind, thoughtful, generous, but just a bit, well, dull. Did I fall in love with him or did I drift into this easy life? It feels like I'm sitting in my favourite chair or resting my head on a soft pillow – it's all very comfortable but not exactly exciting. Our sex life, certainly, has never reached dizzying heights. Pleasant, yes; satisfying, mostly; but never what you'd call urgent or passionate. Maybe it's me. Maybe I don't bring out the animal instinct in Keith. Maybe we're both just too polite.

The loud knocking on the bathroom door brings me back to reality.

'Mum, are you going to be much longer? Dad's up and he sounds like he's on the warpath. You need to come and calm him down.'

I lever myself out of the bath and grab one of the warm towels.

'Thank you, Sophie, I'm coming now. I'll be out in five minutes.'

At least my hangover has gone.

NINE

1987 – STEVE

I sit in the car listening to the tick of the engine as it cools down. The roof's down and the early morning sun is already warm on my face. I get out, light a cigarette and lean against the door.

Shit! I think, *Ali is going to be so mad. What on earth made me drive off like that?* What made me do it was the fact I was pissed off; pissed off with everybody, but mostly pissed off with myself. It's been the story of my life. I achieve something good, like getting an audition for a band, and then I screw it up by doing something stupid, like getting drunk or slagging off someone. Like the time I got invited to join The Works. They were already being talked about as the next Cream. Sid, their drummer, had heard me playing at the Half Moon in Putney. Seems their guy on lead guitar had broken his leg and couldn't tour, so would I like to take his place? Would I like to! It was the chance of a lifetime, well, of my life so far anyway. So, what happens? We play a couple of warm-up gigs before our planned departure to Germany and then I go and get pissed at one of the clubs, get into a fight and then get myself arrested. Sid decides I'm a liability and pulls the plug on me. They decide that "broken leg" can play after all and off they go. Next thing I hear, they're huge in the States and making a fortune.

That's the kind of luck that gets you feeling pretty low about yourself, not to say gives you a reputation for being "unreliable". Sure, I get by giving lessons and playing the odd gig here and there, enough to pay the rent, but I was never offered such a big break again. I know I come across as being a bit intense, something of a loner, not "one of the lads". I can't help it. My sister thinks I'm probably autistic or bipolar or some other new condition she's just read about. No one seems to realise that I'm just uncomfortable around other people. Call it a lack of confidence or just good old-fashioned shyness. Either way, it's the reason I get drunk or high; enough to make me sociable, or too much to get me into trouble. Like last night, for example. I admit I'd smoked a couple of spliffs before we went on stage, so I *was* high, but only enough to take the edge off performing with Keith. Alison got into a groove straight away, but then she's a semi-pro; Dave was laying down a good, steady beat, and Marco was sounding pretty cool, as usual. But Keith, jumping up and down, waving his arm around like Pete Townsend, showing off to his business mates – what a tosser!

I just had to turn my back and ignore him, something I'd always done anyway, and concentrate on my own role. Falling off the stage was not part of the plan. I was trying to catch Dave's eye to start my solo when my foot caught one of the amps, and over I went. Actually, it bloody hurt, even though I was smiling as I fell down. It felt like I was in slow motion, still hanging onto a chord as I hit the floor.

Of course, that stopped everything; the music sliding to a halt, Keith swearing at me, my wrist painful as I tried to stand up, Dave trying to help.

I spent the rest of the evening drifting from one room to another, not really engaging with any particular group of people. I remember sitting outside on a wall for a long time, smoking and observing the guests, feeling quite mellow. A nice woman brought a beer and sat next to me for a while, wanted to know if I was okay, said she had seen me playing in a pub once, surprised I wasn't better known. Tell me about it! Then she said she used to be a nurse and maybe she could take a look at my wrist. Well, one thing led to another and we ended up in my room (Ali always kept one for me, *just in case*, she said). Afterwards, Sarah, the kind nurse lady, fell asleep, but I was wide awake. I felt the need for fresh air. I knew there'd be a scene in the morning, another row between Keith and Ali with me as the main topic of discussion. I guess I just wanted to put some distance between me and them. That's when I took the car. I knew it was Ali's present, but the key was in it and I just got in and drove.

I get back in and look around. I'm in an empty car park overlooking the sea. I've no idea where I am. I decide to drive out and look for a road sign. When I find one, I check in the glove box for a map. Jesus! I'm sixty miles from Ali's. I must have driven for two hours without knowing. Now I have a choice. Do I just keep driving, where to I haven't worked out, or do I turn around and go back? I decide I should return to face the music. Ali will be worried about me, I know. Keith will be fuming about the car; that I know too. I slip the car into drive and head back slowly.

I pull up next to the catering van. Ali is on the steps talking to some people. When she sees me, she rushes over and pulls open the door. 'Jesus, Steve, what's the matter with you? Where have you been?'

I can see the concern on her face and immediately feel guilty for upsetting her. 'I'm okay, Sis, really. I just needed to get out of here. I'm sorry. I didn't mean to take your car.'

'Never mind that,' she says, 'I've been worried sick ever since Marcus told me. I imagined you having an accident somewhere. Driving was never your strong point.'

I give her a rueful smile and squeeze her hand. 'Look, not a scratch on it! You'll love driving it.'

Just as we turn towards the house, Keith comes charging up looking like Mr Angry.

'For fuck's sake, Steve. What on earth were you thinking of taking Ali's car like that? No permission, no insurance! Do you realise how much...?' I can see he's about to say how much Ali's present cost him but manages to stop himself in time. Instead, he looks at the BMW, trying to see if there's any damage. Satisfied there's nothing obvious, he begins to calm down. He looks at Ali, then me. 'This situation can't go on. You're a bloody liability. The party is definitely over.'

Ali grips my hand harder. 'Don't be so mean, Keith. You always said there was a place for him here.'

'For Christ's sake, Ali. I know he's your brother and you feel responsible for him, or sorry for him, more likely, but it's time he stood on his own two feet. We can't keep bailing him out.' And with that, he storms off down the drive.

Ali and I are still holding hands, watching him. 'Don't worry about him, he'll calm down by tonight.'

'No, he's probably right,' I say. 'I should move on. It's not fair on you.'

'But I like having you here,' she says, 'the kids do too.'

I smile at her. 'Another reason for leaving. Keith probably thinks I'm a bad influence on them as well.'

'But where will you go? What will you do?'

'Don't worry about me. I'll be all right. Something will turn up.'

She leans forward and kisses me on the cheek. 'Come on,' she says, 'let's get you something to eat. You must be starving.'

TEN

1992

That was the last time I saw any of them for a long while. After breakfast, I'd packed my stuff and Ali drove me to the station. We hugged each other on the platform then she pushed some notes into the top pocket of my jacket. 'That'll keep you going for a few days until you sort yourself out. I'm sorry it's not more.'

I squeezed her harder. Over her shoulder, I could see the train approaching. 'Thanks, Sis. I'm sorry I've been such a pain. It's me should be looking after you, not the other around.'

She pulled back and smiled, wiping a tear from her cheek. 'Yeah, that'll be the day.'

Ali stood on the platform as the train pulled away. I stayed at the window and watched her waving until we turned a bend and I could see her no more. Not for the first time in my life, I felt really alone.

Gazing out of the window, watching the landscape rush by, I tried to figure out what I was going to do next.

The arrival of the drinks trolley interrupted my thoughts. Normally, I wouldn't get anything but this time I asked for a can of beer. I reached into my pocket for some money and found the notes Ali had stuffed there. *Christ, there must be over a hundred quid!* I thought. I shoved a note in the direction of the lady and waited for her to hand over the beer and the change. Opening the can, I took a long swig and counted the money slowly. Ali had given me 150 pounds, enough to keep me going for a couple of weeks at least. 'Thanks, Ali,' I murmured to myself, 'you're a star.'

I get back to the flat in Kilburn I share with Andy and Kate. When I say "share", I mean it was really their flat and they let me rent the spare room, like a lodger. I'd met Andy in The Greyhound; we'd both gone to check out a band and got talking about music. Turned out he was writing for one of the music papers and was doing the round of pubs. He said it was a good way to find new talent, to see what they sounded like and how they were going down with the punters. We bumped into each other a few times after that. He even came to see me whenever I got asked to the odd gig, so when he mentioned that his lodger was moving and would I be interested in moving in, I jumped at the chance. I'd spent too long dossing around at various places, usually someone's I'd played with who was going on the road for a month or two. The idea of a more permanent arrangement appealed to me a lot. Especially with someone who seemed to have the same musical tastes as me. And Kate was lovely. She was a stylist for a photographer and often worked in the evenings. I think she was pleased that Andy had someone to share his music gigs with.

'So, how did it go?' asks Kate, handing me a mug of tea.

'Don't ask,' I grimace. 'It was a disaster. I had a major bust- up with Keith and left my sister in tears.' I decide not to mention the car incident.

'Oh, no, sounds awful.' Her soft Scottish accent somehow made it sound even more sympathetic.

It was Kate who eventually played a major part in getting my life back on track. About three months after I'd said goodbye to my sister, the three of us were out one night, listening to a band, when she introduced me to a friend of hers, Gloria, a dark-eyed, dark-haired girl from Brazil. Kate had met her at a photographer's working as his assistant, and they'd quickly struck up a friendship. It turned out she was trying to establish herself as a singer/songwriter – playing a few gigs at one of the clubs in Soho that put on Brazilian nights. I thought she was stunning; her warm smile and friendly eyes had the effect of making me feel relaxed, less unsure of myself. We chatted in between listening to the band. Kate had already told her I was something of a musician; we began to explore each other's tastes in music, past and present. When I offered to buy more drinks, I was amused that she wanted a Guinness, but she explained it was a taste she'd acquired in London. I couldn't help noticing that the darkness of the beer matched the colour of her eyes. As the band began to pack up and we finished our drinks, I could feel myself blushing as I told her I hoped we'd meet again. She took my hand in both of hers, smiled and said simply, 'Me too.'

On the way home, Kate wanted to know if I'd asked Gloria for her phone number. 'Idiot,' she said, when I told her I'd forgotten to do that. The next day, she gave me the number. 'Call her,' she said, pushing the paper towards me. 'I'm sure she'd like to see you again.' Encouraged by this prompting, I called her that evening and we arranged to meet at another gig. From that night on, we began to see each other more often, usually to listen to live music, but sometimes to visit a gallery or museum or just a walk in the park. I remember the first time I saw her perform at one of her Brazilian clubs and how amazed I was at the range of her voice and the emotion she put into singing the haunting Portuguese *fado* or gentle *bossa novas*. I could tell from the reaction of the audience that she was bringing the authentic sounds of her country to this small stage in London. The end of every song was greeted by a brief moment of silence before enthusiastic applause broke out.

When she finished her set, she came over and sat next to me. She told me she'd felt a bit nervous performing in front of me, but her eyes continued to shine with the passion of her music. I told her she was great, of course, and how much I'd loved listening to her, especially the songs she'd written herself. That night, she came back with me to my room at Kate and Andy's and we made love for the first time.

From that moment, we became what Kate teasingly described as a "musical item". Gloria moved in with me soon after and our life together developed a regular routine. I continued to give guitar lessons and play the occasional pub gig. Gloria worked at the photographer's and sang at her Brazilian club nights. Most evenings and at weekends, we would enjoy experimenting with our own music. Borrowing her acoustic guitar, I began to accompany her as she sang, quickly picking up the rhythm of her music. By now, Gloria was writing new songs, introducing elements of her experiences of life in London. One evening, I picked up my electric guitar and began to add a few "blue" notes to one of her songs. She frowned at first but then began to see how the mix of her traditional song structure with my harder- edged sound really worked well together. We experimented with more songs until we had a collection of material that excited us.

We began thinking about recording some of the music; we just needed to scrape enough money together to buy some studio time and make a demo.

We were very happy together. For the first time in my life, I felt comfortable and secure in a relationship; the tensions and anger I had lived with for so long melted the moment Gloria walked through the door. Sunday mornings, I'd leave her in bed, nip out for the paper and a couple of croissants, make some coffee and prepare a breakfast in bed for two.

'Didn't you say you once played in a band, a long time ago?' She drew out "a long time ago", gently teasing me about the gap in our ages, she being twelve years younger than me.

'Well, yeah, but it was amateur stuff. Saturday nights in sports clubs and church halls playing pop songs.'

'But you enjoyed it, yes?'

'No, not really. My sister was in the band too, so I could keep an eye on her. But I guess it was good practice. I was happy just to turn up, play and get paid.'

'And you don't see the band anymore?'

I began to tell her about Alison's birthday party, how I fell off the stage, how I "borrowed" Ali's present from Keith, how it was the last time I saw my sister. Gloria lay next to me, saying nothing, gently stroking my chest. She knew what it was like to be separated from your family, although in her case it was distance, not dramas, that made it difficult.

Suddenly I sat up in bed. 'Jesus, why didn't I think of it before? Marco!'

'Who is Marco?' said Gloria, sweeping crumbs from the sheets and retrieving bits of the paper from the floor.

'He was our singer; quite good really and not a bad bloke.'

'And why do you think of him now?'

'Because he works in advertising, making TV commercials, at least I think he still does. He must know some people with a recording studio.' I pulled her towards me and kissed her. 'I'll find a way to get hold of him tomorrow and see if he can help.' Gloria smiled and pressed her warm body along the length of mine. We made love, the sun beaming through the window, filtered by the leaves of the trees across the street.

It took a while to find Marcus but eventually I tracked him down to an agency in Mayfair. He couldn't have been friendlier and offered to help us find a studio with some spare recording time. (He didn't tell me this until years later, but he actually booked the time himself then pretended to cancel it, giving us a "free" three hours.)

Gloria and I managed to find a bass player and drummer who were willing to work for next to nothing. We arranged to meet at the studio in Soho and Marcus surprised me by turning up too. Three hours wasn't a huge amount of time, but we'd decided in advance which songs we wanted to record, and Marco proved to have a talent for producing. He had a good ear for the music and the sound we wanted to create, directing the sound engineer to focus on the emotion in Gloria's voice. By the time our three hours were up, we'd managed to record and mix four tracks to our satisfaction. We left the studio on a high, clutching a cassette of the tracks, and treated everyone to tea and bacon sarnies at an all-night café.

About three weeks later, Marcus called me at the flat. 'Hey, Steve, how's it going? Done anything with that cassette yet?'

'Not really, apart from play it a lot. We were thinking of sending it to one of Gloria's cousins in Brazil.'

'I think we can do better than that, old mate.'

'What do you mean?'

'Well, I kept a copy myself and played it to a few people I know in the record business. I've just had a call from a guy who wants to meet you and Gloria. How're you fixed on Friday?'

It took a moment or two for my mind to process this information. 'I guess so, I'll have to ask her. Who is this guy?'

'He runs a label for international artists. I think you'll like him.'

'Jesus, Marco, I don't know what to say. It sounds brilliant! I can't wait to tell Gloria.'

He gave me the address of an office in Kensington and arranged to meet us there. After the call from Marcus, I sat and played the tape again, my mind exploring a whole bunch of possibilities. By the time Gloria came in, I was bursting to tell her about my conversation with Marco. At first, she thought I was pulling her leg, but her face told a different story. Then we hugged and kissed each other and did a little dance around the bedroom.

Gerry, the record label guy, greeted us in his office, offering cups of tea or coffee, then sat behind his desk and smiled. 'Gloria, I really like the tape Marcus sent me. I think you have a beautiful voice and the music is terrific, traditional but modern at the same time. I don't know how much Marcus has told you, but I specialise in distributing music from overseas artists who have the potential to break into the UK and Europe. However,' he paused to light a cigarette and exhale a plume of smoke, 'in your case, you're already here! And I believe we could export you. I'm thinking particularly Brazil, it's a big market.'

I sat there listening to Gerry and getting the distinct feeling he was only talking to Gloria. She must have picked up the same vibe because she reached over to hold my hand, giving it a reassuring squeeze.

'You are very kind, Mr Gerry,' she said, 'but it's not just me. We made this music together. The sound you say you like so much was Steve's idea.'

Gerry glanced over at Marcus and shifted in his chair, looking uncomfortable.

'You're right, of course. It's a wonderful collaboration and Steve deserves full credit. But,' he paused again and leant forward on his desk, 'I'm in the business of selling records and my feeling, my *professional* feeling, is that we have a better chance of success if we can package you as a solo artist.'

I remember flinching at the *package* word. I didn't think Gloria would appreciate being wrapped up and presented as some kind of attractive parcel. She looked at me, searching my face for a response. I could tell from the look in her eyes that part of her wanted to remain loyal to me as her musical partner; but I could see another emotion too: pure ambition. The room fell silent for a while. Then Marcus spoke up. 'Look, Steve, we all know you and Gloria made this music together but what Gerry says makes sense. If you want to reach a bigger audience, it will be a lot easier if Gloria is presented as a solo artist. But the overriding interest will be in the unique sound coming from the collaboration between her and a British musician, that's you, mate; we can call it a fusion.'

I couldn't help smiling, listening to Marco. No wonder he'd made such a successful career in advertising.

'You're right,' I said, 'it makes sense to focus on Gloria. Besides, I never really enjoyed being in the spotlight.'

I felt the room breathe a collective sigh of relief. Gerry was back in relaxed mode and began making plans, although not before outlining a basic recording contract.

Again, Marcus came to the rescue, helping out with percentages and publishing rights until we had a deal that suited everyone. Gerry promised to send our demo to his contacts in Brazil to test the water. We agreed that if he got a positive response, we'd go back and re-record the tracks, only this time with the luxury of more studio time and a couple of extra musicians. We all smiled and shook hands. Afterwards, Gloria and I took Marco to the nearest pub and bought him several large drinks; we both knew we couldn't have done it without him.

Life returned to normal except we now had a kind of nervous anticipation waiting for news from Brazil. A couple of months went by; the excitement began to fade and we began to wonder if Gerry's "contacts" were not so hot after all.

    I remember it clearly. It was a warm Tuesday night in June when the phone rang.

    'Hi, Steve? It's Gerry. I've got some good news for you and your lovely lady.' I motioned to Gloria to come over to the phone and listen. 'I've just been speaking to one of the label managers in Rio. He loves the music and wants to meet you. He thinks the demo is good enough to release and wants you out there to do some publicity. I told him we'd prefer to re-record the tracks but he said come out anyway so he can introduce you to the TV and radio stations – he'll even pay for your flights. How could I say no! What do you think?'

    We looked at each other, smiling and nodding at the same time. 'Yes, yes, that sounds great, Gerry. When would he want us to go?'

    'Soon, I guess,' said Gerry. 'Leave that to me and I'll be in touch. Just make sure your passports are up to date, okay?'

He hung up and we hugged and did another little dance around the room. 'You are going to be fantastic, I just know it,' I said, kissing her neck and squeezing her tight.

'No,' said Gloria, stroking my face, 'we both are.'

A year later, the EP had been released first in Brazil and then Portugal. We'd agreed on the one-word name "Gloria"; whether it was Gloria performing as an artist by herself or on stage alongside me and the other musicians. We liked the way it became a symbol for a collective, inclusive group of talented people.

We travelled twice to Brazil promoting the record and performing live on TV and at several venues across the country. Nothing too big – no big stadia – but building a strong audience through word of mouth. In between time, we went back to the studio to work on new material for our first album. Money was starting to come in from the EP and Gerry had negotiated an advance from the label manager in Brazil. It meant we could give up our day jobs and concentrate on the music. Throughout the year, we'd continued to "lodge" with Kate and Andy, but we began to think more and more about getting a place of our own.

'How about we move somewhere warmer?' suggested Gloria as we lay in bed listening to the radio one morning.

'What, you mean Brazil?' My voice must have registered a note of concern.

'No, although that would be nice for me, but it's too far away. We need to be closer to London. I was thinking maybe France or Spain or even Italy.'

We lay there for a while lost in our own thoughts. Then I leant over and kissed her. 'I know just the place.'

'Really? So where are you taking me?' She smiled and looked excited.

'To Spain, a place called Cunit, you'll love it.'

Three days later, Gloria told me softly, gently, and with rising degrees of wonder and excitement that she was pregnant.

I admit my first reaction was shock, quickly followed by panic and the feeling my life was about to change forever. But none of this I conveyed to her. Instead, I smiled and pulled her towards me. 'That's fantastic news. You're going to be as wonderful a mother as you are a performer. Come on, let's go and tell Kate. It'll be another good reason for moving out!'

ELEVEN

2007 – DAVE

'David!' I can hear my mother calling. It's ten in the morning and she's still in bed. I think about turning up the volume on the radio so I can pretend I didn't hear her, but I know she'll carry on calling until I go up. Instead, I re-boil the kettle and make some tea.

'Oh, David, you're such a good boy,' she says as I enter her room. 'How did you know I wanted tea?'

Because you always want one at this time, you old fraud, I thought, but didn't say.

Ever since my father left us when I was fifteen, she's relied on me, heavily. Some might say dominated. At the beginning, I was happy to be the "man" of the house; running errands, doing chores, keeping the garden tidy while she cooked me interesting meals and kept up a constant tirade about "him". Lucky man, I think now, he escaped her endless criticism and suffocating neediness.

Her changing moods got worse when I went to uni. At a time when I was hoping to build some kind of social life, maybe join a band, go to parties, get drunk, have sex, her phone calls increased. Could I come home because 'the dustman hadn't been', 'the neighbour's cat was messing in the garden', 'the washing machine wouldn't work'? I realise Oxford was only fifty miles from Northwood and in theory I could get back in a couple of hours, but mentally I wished there was a million miles between us.

It was Keith who asked me at school if I wanted to join "his" band.

I was already in the cadet corps and had developed an interest in playing percussion in the school orchestra. My errant father, on a rare visit and probably out of a sense of guilt, gave me the money to buy my first drum kit. I set it up in the garden shed, hanging some old blankets on the walls for soundproofing. I wouldn't say they were "heroes", but my drumming influences at the time were people like Ginger Baker and Charlie Watts, not the exaggerated showmanship of Keith Moon. If I had to name one man who I thought was the best, it would have to be the American Gene Krupa – showman, yes, but brilliant at pounding the drums for minutes at a time with amazing solos. I would spend hours after school and at weekends practising until I became, even if I say it myself, pretty good. Good enough for Keith to ask me to join him.

I enjoyed playing in the band, especially when we practised round at Keith's. For one thing, it got me out of the house and away from Mother for a few hours. Our Saturday gigs were even better; an early evening meet-up then off to the venue, a couple of beers and a late-night return home. Of course, I'd pay for it the next day, she telling me how selfish I was to abandon her, and making me take her out for a "little ride" in the car. (I'd passed my test first time as soon as I'd turned seventeen, something I was rather proud of.) I'd end up driving aimlessly around the Chilterns, listening to her prattling on about people she used to know and who 'never come to visit me anymore.' *Because you're a whining, bitter old woman,* I felt like screaming, but instead I'd gradually increase the volume of the radio to drown out her litany of complaints and criticisms.

I met Sarah at Oxford. I was in my final year reading physics and she'd just started a law degree. We were both in the same pub listening to a band who thought they might be the next Rolling Stones – something, in my estimation, that was far beyond their ability. Sarah was returning from the bar, attempting to carry three drinks in two hands when she bumped into me. Correction, barged into me just as I was about to take a sip of beer, causing me to bash my teeth against the rim of the glass and tip beer down the front of my shirt. The middle of the three drinks, a strange purple concoction – I found out later it was vodka and blackcurrant – splashed over the sleeve of my corduroy jacket.

'Oh, I'm so sorry,' she exclaimed in a very posh accent. 'Someone pushed me. It's so crowded in here. I do apologise.'

I looked at the sleeve then turned to look up at her; she must have been a good four inches taller than me. I took in the nice hair, the kind eyes behind the black frame of her glasses and the look of utmost concern on her face. My anger quickly faded away, even as the sticky drink dripped down onto my wrist. 'It's not a problem, really. I never liked this jacket much anyway.'

She smiled. 'You must let me buy you another drink. Hold these and I'll go back to the bar.'

'No,' I said, 'I think it might be safer if I go. Where are your friends? I'll find you.'

Even after several months of seeing each other, I was never quite sure what Sarah saw in me. Maybe it was because I was the opposite of most of the men she knew – posh chaps who oozed confidence except when it came to girls, then reverted to schoolboy jokes and behaviour. 'All very tiresome' as she would say, 'and so immature.' Perhaps the absence of my father's attitude towards women, or possibly the influence of my mother, made me more in tune with the female mind. Whatever the reason, or reasons, we continued to seek out each other's company throughout that year, taking it in turns to find interesting or amusing things to do as a distraction from our studies. We began to have sex, too. Tentatively at first – neither of us was very experienced – but gradually finding a shared experience that suited us; not wildly passionate, but deeply satisfying.

I'd rigged up a small camping stove in the bedroom of my lodgings so I didn't have to go into the communal kitchen to make myself a hot drink. Sarah and I would prop ourselves up on pillows, sipping coffee, and talk about our chosen subjects; me explaining the scientific life of a thunderstorm, while she described the subtle differences between defence and prosecution. They were wonderful times, only spoilt by phone calls from home. Sarah would often volunteer to come with me; she thought it was very kind of me to be so attentive to my mother. But the last thing I needed was Mother casting her critical eye over my girlfriend and finding her 'not suitable for her son.'

After I graduated, we didn't see each other so often. I was settling into my new job at the Met Office and Sarah was studying hard for her finals. But we kept in touch and I would drive to Oxford as often as possible, booking a room in a hotel by the river and spending the weekend with her. It was during one of these visits, walking hand in hand after dinner along the riverbank, that I asked Sarah to marry me. I'd made up my mind to ask her some weeks before but wanted to wait for the right moment. I knew I was in love with her and worried that if I didn't ask her now she might go off into the world of law and meet someone else. I must admit it unnerved me when she giggled at first but then she realised I was serious and said nothing for a while. I thought, *Dave, mate, you've blown it,* but then she smiled, lowered her head to kiss me and said, 'Yes, yes please.' I could hardly believe it. I felt as if I was walking on air and couldn't stop smiling. I gave her a big hug and picked her up as best I could and whirled her around. 'Does this mean I get to meet your mother at last?' she teased. Even the thought of it could do nothing to cast a dark cloud over my happiness.

As expected, Mother's reception over tea one afternoon was polite but frosty. I could see she was impressed by the flowers and homemade cakes Sarah had brought for her, but she wasn't quite ready to give her "approval". But, gradually, under the gentle openness of Sarah's questions and her interest in the replies, she began to visibly soften, although she couldn't resist an opportunity to scold me for 'not introducing me to this delightful young lady sooner.' It helped that Sarah came from a fairly wealthy background. I could tell this would appeal to my mother's suburban snobbishness; something she would have been dying to tell her friends, if she had any.

The wedding took place a few months later. Neither of us wanted a big "do" and Sarah's parents were happy to host a reception in the grounds of the family home. I invited Keith and Alison, fresh from their own recent wedding, and Marcus agreed to be my best man. I sent an invite to Steve too, but I wasn't surprised he never replied. Apart from Mother and a couple of friends from work, that was the extent of my invitations. It didn't even cross my mind to tell my father, even if I'd known where he lived, something I had no intention of finding out.

We spent our honeymoon on a walking holiday in the Bavarian Alps then settled down to married life in the flat we bought in Hampstead. Sarah was keen to pursue her legal career and had taken up the offer of a position with one of the leading legal firms while she studied for her bar exams. My work at the Met Office kept me busy, and I began to gain a reputation in my specialised field of storms, enough to send me away to several conferences at home and abroad. From time to time, Sarah and I talked about having children, but we were both caught up in our own careers and relished our weekends and holidays together, selfishly enjoying each other's company, unhampered by babies.

Things changed when Sarah turned thirty. By then, she had qualified as a barrister with an increasing amount of work in divorce law. Female lawyers were still uncommon, so it was not surprising she was sought out by a high percentage of women clients. I never did work out what happened to make her suddenly want to have children – it would have been less surprising if she'd said she never wanted to have children, having seen the effects that a messy divorce could have on the offspring of warring parents.

A year went by, but nothing happened. To begin with, we weren't too concerned, but after another year without getting pregnant, Sarah started to get anxious, thinking there was something wrong with her. We took medical advice; trying sex in the best position to conceive, or on the most likely day of the month, even following a special "stimulating" diet, but to no avail. It all became quite clinical and our sex life diminished as Sarah's disappointment increased. As it turned out, there was nothing wrong with her at all; she was completely healthy, glowingly fertile. It was me. It seems I had a low sperm count and was unlikely to be able to father a child.

It was the beginning of the end. Our lives began to separate, each concentrating on our individual careers. Then, one evening, Sarah came home and told me she'd met someone else, another barrister, and asked me for a divorce. My mind went back to the start of our relationship and my astonishment that she ever wanted to go out with me in the first place. Naturally, I was sad to lose her, but a large part of me – well, my rational side anyway – felt I'd been lucky to have been with her at all. After the divorce, I never saw or heard from her again, until one year I got a Christmas card with a photo enclosed of her holding a baby. I don't know whether she wanted me to see that she'd finally been successful in her desire for a child, that somehow I'd be happy for her. Maybe, in the glow of motherhood, she hadn't realised that all it would do was remind me of the reason we split up in the first place. My mother, predictably, said '"that woman" was never good enough for you to start with.' I know it was supposed to make me feel better, that now we both knew what it was like to be "deserted", but I was determined not to inherit her bitterness.

I stayed in the flat for a year or two but when Mother had the first of her mini-strokes, I decided it was easier to move back "home". I know it sounds a bit lame, grown man returns to live with parent, but it was a lot simpler than travelling to and fro, waiting for the next pleading phone call. At least I made a good profit on the sale of the flat, enough to put some savings in the bank and buy a decent car.

I stand at the foot of the stairs, hand on the bannister, listening. 'I'm off now,' I shout. 'I'm meeting Marcus for lunch, be back later.'

'Bye, dear,' comes the rather doleful reply. 'Have a nice time.'

TWELVE

1972 — KEITH

Sitting by a window in The Barley Mow, pint in one hand, cigarette in the other, glancing at my watch for about the fifth time; it's still only 8pm. I'm beginning to wonder where the hell they are, this is supposed to be my *stag* do, when I spot Marco and Dave pushing through the pub door.

'Sorry we're late, mate,' says Marco. 'We had a couple of calls to make. Is anyone else coming? Where's Steve?'

They've both got stupid grins on their faces as if they've had a few drinks already or they're planning something I don't know about or probably won't like.

'God knows! I did tell him, but you know what he's like. He's probably forgotten. I've asked a couple of chaps from the office but if they're not here in half an hour, I suggest we move on. What's the plan?'

'Well,' says Dave, 'we thought a drink or two here, then on to a meal and then move on...'

'Move on where?' A note of suspicion enters my voice. Dave taps his nose with a finger. 'Don't you worry, you'll like it, I promise.' I'm not entirely convinced. I've heard the stories about grooms being chained to lamp posts, or waking up with their arms in plaster, or worse still, waking up in Scotland. At least I'm not getting married in the morning; the wedding's still three days away.

Marco returns from the bar with a tray of drinks – pints and whisky chasers – and we wait to see if anyone else arrives.

By 9pm, and several more drinks later, I'm feeling a lot more relaxed. The guys from the office don't show up but I'm not that bothered. We're not that close; workmates rather than chums. Marco, Dave and I go back a long way and I'm enjoying reminiscing about our school days and life in the band.

We've just agreed we're getting hungry when Steve stumbles through the door. I watch him looking around, then Marco stands up, shouts and waves him over.

'Grab a drink, mate,' says Marco. 'What kept you?' Steve downs a whisky but doesn't offer an explanation, waving the question away while he lights a roll-up. Not for the first time I wonder why he always manages to look so moody. Nor for the first time do I wonder how he and Ali can be so completely different, as if they had different parents or unrelated childhoods.

Dave looks at his watch. 'Drink up, everyone. It's time we got going. We've got a table booked at the Hellenic.'

We amble outside into a warm June evening and head towards Marylebone High Street. The owner of the restaurant greets Marco like an old friend and guides us to a table in the corner. It seems Marco is one of his best customers, his agency being just around the corner. We order food and wine, taking suggestions from the waiter, and continue the conversations we started in the pub.

We're probably getting quite loud as the drinks take

effect, but the noise level soon drops when the food arrives, and we concentrate on eating. I'm hoping the food will soak up some of the alcohol before we "move on", as Dave has intimated.

I'm feeling relaxed and enjoying the company of my best friends. We discuss most of the usual topics – work, music, sport, what's on TV, who had a shag in Cunit. It turns out that Marcus got lucky twice. Steve won't say, although we all know he disappeared most nights to the campsite so probably was successful; poor Dave, none – he spent most of his time off recovering from sunburn or mosquito bites; Alison – doubtful (and as she is soon to be my wife, I feel uncomfortable pursuing that line of enquiry). As for me, I admit to sleeping with Diana, a very nice girl from Brighton who wore a white bikini and seemed to take a shine to me. We laugh and pull each other's legs, all the usual banter.

We move on to some of the more newsworthy issues of the day like the IRA bombings, the striking coal miners, high inflation and the tragic air crash outside Heathrow.

'Can you imagine,' says Dave, 'you get on a plane and five minutes later you're falling out of the sky over Staines?' No one says anything for a few moments.

'Karma,' says Steve, 'could happen to any of us, anytime.'

I watch him toying with his moussaka. He doesn't seem to have eaten very much.

'Yeah, well, thanks for that, Steve,' says Marco. 'Can we go back to talking about the rubbish that's in the charts? Seriously, does anyone really want to listen to Donny Osmond singing about puppy love? I mean, for fuck's sake, what's that all about?'

As usual, Marco has a way of keeping it light-hearted, although the couple at the next table look a bit shocked. Maybe she's a Donny fan. Meanwhile, Dave's waving at the waiter and ordering coffee and *Metaxa* for everyone.

Another round of Greek brandy later, this time on the house, we ask for the bill. Very generously, Marco and Dave agree to split the cost between them, refusing my offer to pay my share and not even bothering to see if Steve might contribute. I mean, I know he's hard up, but it annoys me that he accepts their food and drink but doesn't think of offering to pay anything. Marco and Dave, on the other hand, seem to ignore his reluctance – bad manners I would call it – as if it's normal Steve behaviour. I decide, out of respect for Ali and her parents, that this is not the night to pick a fight. Instead, I open my wallet and slap a couple of notes on the table, hoping the large tip might embarrass him, but he seems oblivious to the hint.

Outside on the pavement, Marco is hailing a cab. He gives the driver an address in Soho and we pile in. Ten minutes later, we get out in Brewer Street and Marco is leading us down an alley, stopping outside a nondescript doorway with no name or number. At this point, despite the relaxing effect of the booze, I'm beginning to feel nervous again. Marco rings the discreet bell and a few moments later the door is opened by a large guy in a black suit who waves him inside. The other two find a way to nudge me through a beaded curtain and into a dimly lit room where I'm greeted by a young woman; a young, attractive, topless woman. It's not that I haven't seen topless women before, there were plenty on the beach in Spain, but never have I seen one in a bar holding a tray of drinks. 'Hi, I'm Brandy,' she says, handing me a glass of something sparkling which, even in my bemused state, I decide is probably not champagne. 'You must be Keith, congratulations.'

I find myself struggling to look her in the eye and not look at her breasts. 'Thanks,' I manage to blurt, opting to focus on a point between her neck and bare shoulder.

We're led to a small alcove with a banquette and round

table and Brandy brings over another tray of drinks and, rather surprisingly, a plate of ham sandwiches. They look totally out of place in these surroundings but, as Marcus explains later, the club cannot sell drinks without offering some food to go with them.

Looking back, it all seemed so naïve, so innocent. There were no strippers, no lap dances, no suggestion of other "services". Just tables of mainly businessmen being waited on by pretty topless girls, like Brandy. But at the time, I suppose, it was considered to be quite daring – London's first topless bar.

It's nearly midnight when Dave announces he's going home; he's got an early start in the morning. Steve takes the opportunity to grab a cab with Dave and mumbles his excuses. Considering the amount he's had to drink, he still looks remarkably sober. The pair of them head for the door, Dave weaving slightly and wishing me good luck for the big day ahead.

Marcus slides up to me on the seat, puts his arm round my shoulder and clinks his glass to mine.

'So, tell me, Keith,' his words are slurred and his eyes look bleary, 'how on earth did you manage to snaffle such a gorgeous girl as Ali?' I smile but don't say anything for a while. I'm not going to admit it to Marco, but the same thought has crossed my mind many times – what exactly does she see in me?

I ruffle his shaggy hair. 'Well, mate,' I say, 'fucked if I know. Maybe I'm just a lucky bastard! Come on, time to take me home. You're my best man, supposed to be looking after me!'

We stagger out of the club arm in arm and Marco hails a cab.

I may have seen bare tits on my stag night but at least no one tied me to a lamp post, for which I breathe a huge sigh of relief.

THIRTEEN

1982

It's our tenth wedding anniversary and I'm taking Ali out to dinner. My secretary has booked a table at L'Ecu de France; Ali and I are going to spend the night in a hotel in town while her mother looks after the children at home.

Supposed to be going out. It's 6.30 and I'm still at the office on the phone to the publisher of a motoring magazine. I'm trying to decide whether to buy it or start one of my own. I may not have been the brightest guy at school but I'm good at spotting a trend – and taking a risk. I've seen how the classified ads in my free newspapers are always loaded with columns of cars for sale and I've figured how to turn this into a nationwide platform. Eventually, the guy names his price and I tell him I'll give him an answer in the morning. Then I'm on the phone quickly to Ali.

'Darling, I'm really sorry but I'm only just leaving the office. I think it's best if you get a cab into town and I'll meet you at the restaurant. I'll get Jenny to move the booking back and see you there at eight.' I hear the sigh of frustration coming down the phone, the sound that says this isn't the first time I've mucked up our plans.

'Okay,' she says, 'Mum's already here so I'll phone for a cab, but it's going to cost a fortune!'

Back in the day when the freesheets started, people were surprised when I gave up a good job to join one of the new breed of local papers. But I loved the idea of starting something new, of challenging tradition. My role as marketing manager gave me every opportunity to explore innovative ways to promote the paper. Local commercial radio stations had just started broadcasting and proved to be the ideal medium for drumming up business. Airtime was cheap and the audience loved the idea of local news mixed with pop music and chat. Our message was simple – their local freesheet was the best marketplace to buy and sell anything. It caught on, quickly. Soon we were publishing freesheets all around the Home Counties, and the revenues were rolling in. Within two years, I'd been promoted to managing director, by which time we had over fifty titles and I'd been rewarded with a minor share in the business. Of course, it wasn't long before the owners of the national papers saw the freesheets not as a threat to their hold on the news but as lucrative sources of revenue. So, when my boss, the owner of the publishing company, saw the large sum being dangled in front of his eyes, it didn't take him long to accept the offer. And I made a sizeable chunk of money myself. The new owner didn't really need me to run the company, the business model was well established, so I accepted their kind offer to buy out my contract and decided there was only one person I wanted to work for: myself.

With some seed money from my previous, now wealthy, boss, plus most of what I had, I started AK Publishing. We began with a couple of glossy county-style magazines. I'd reasoned that if the freesheets were popular with the punters then they might go for something a bit more upmarket, with fashion, restaurant reviews, homes for sale and news of local celebrities. The magazines were well received to begin with – people were used to having to pay for this style of magazine – but it was hard work drumming up the advertising revenue. My staff had to spend a lot of time talking on the phone, and the monthly issue date put off most of the customers for small ads.

It didn't take me long to realise the county magazines had become something of a vanity project. I'd taken my eye of the prize, the prize being the cash generated by the classified ads.

It didn't take a genius to work out that "motors for sale" was the most popular element in the freesheets. What I needed to do was merge the idea of classified ads for cars within a magazine format – then publish it nationally, which is how I came to be talking to the owner of a motoring magazine on my wedding anniversary. I couldn't wait to tell Ali.

I find her sitting at the bar in the restaurant. With her slim figure and straight black hair she still looks like the eighteen-year-old who played in the band. I stand in the doorway for a few moments, admiring, before joining her at the bar. I touch her gently on the shoulder. "I'm sorry I'm late, darling. Have you been waiting long?"

She turns to face me with a rather cross look on her face. 'I was going to give you until I finished this,' she said, stirring her drink with one of those glass sticks, 'but you're here now, so I can't be angry.' She leans towards me, smiling, and kisses me on the cheek. 'Happy anniversary, husband. What kept you?'

I signal the barman to bring me the same drink as Ali's. 'I've decided to start another magazine!'

'But I thought you said those county mags were too much effort.'

'Ah, but this one is something new. A national magazine to sell used cars, just like the classified ads in the freesheets but bigger.'

'Are you sure that's going to be interesting enough? I mean, will people read it?'

'Well, we'll throw in some editorial, a couple of reviews, some road tests, lots of colour ads, but basically loads of photos of used cars from all over the country.'

'And have you got a name for this masterpiece?' I could tell she was humouring me.

'Sure, I've thought of that already. In fact, I had the name before anything else – I'm going to call it *MotoMart!*

'So, what are you going to tell the chap you were talking to? Are you going to buy his magazine?'

'That's a tricky one. He's got the circulation I need and the major advertisers. He knows that, which is why he's asking a lot for it. On the other hand, with the money I have to spend buying it, I could start my own magazine. It's a bigger risk but exciting too!'

Ali smiles. 'Well, if anyone can make it happen, you can. Let's drink to *MotoMart*, then can we eat? I'm starving!'

I signal to the head waiter, hovering at the end of the bar, and he leads us to our table, sitting us down and unfolding our napkins with a flourish. Two kir royales appear as if by magic. I make a mental note to thank Jenny for telling the restaurant it's our anniversary.

I raise my glass to Ali. 'Happy anniversary, darling. Here's to the next ten years.' She looks at me over the top of her glass with that expression that tells me I don't always know what's going on inside her head, then she gives me a big smile. 'Let's just take one year at a time.'

After our meal, we walk to the hotel off Baker Street,

have a nightcap at the bar, go to our room feeling slightly drunk, get into bed and have the best sex we've had in a long while; the kind you can only have when your kids are out of the way. We cuddle up and kiss goodnight. Before I drift off to sleep, I think again about *MotoMart* and make my decision; I bloody well will start my own magazine!

FOURTEEN

1999 – MARCUS

I pick up the post on my way in from walking the dog and climb the stairs to the flat. After I've fed Lola, I switch on my latest gadget, an Italian coffee maker, and carefully measure out the correct amount of coffee. While I wait for the machine to do its thing, I sort through the post; amongst the junk mail and a couple of bills there's an expensive-looking envelope addressed by hand.

I don't recognise the writing and wonder who it could be from. These days, more and more people are communicating by email; it's instant and easy, but I still get a nostalgic pleasure when I receive a "real" letter.

I pour the coffee, sit at the kitchen table and slit open the envelope. There's a card inside from Keith and Ali inviting me to spend some time with them at their villa in Provence. I'm a bit surprised as I haven't heard from either of them for a while. I remember reading in the business section of *The Sunday Times* that Keith had sold some of his interests in publishing and exhibitions and was now concentrating on his internet businesses, so I'm guessing he could work from anywhere.

It suggests a couple of weeks in July and there's a jaunty PS, leaving it open if I "want to bring someone", so I assume Ali wrote the card. It wouldn't be Keith's style to invite someone he didn't know.

July wouldn't be a problem. Since I left the agency – a mutually satisfactory arrangement – and started working as a consultant, I can be selective about when and how I work. Although the royalties from the mobile phone jingle dried up a while ago, there's still plenty of work out there, whether writing commercials or composing.

I can't remember the last time I had a proper two-week holiday. Lots of weekends away, certainly, but I'm not one for going off on my own or joining in with a group. I like to see people I know, but find a long weekend is usually enough. It would be great to see Ali again, but I'm not so sure I relish the idea of two weeks with Keith; he can be a tad overbearing. However, the idea of spending time in Provence, a region I've always been fond of, begins to sound very attractive.

I turn on the laptop to check my diary; there's absolutely nothing that far ahead. Lola won't be a problem, either. Fanny, in the garden flat below, has always been happy to look after her since her own dogs had to be put down. I shift into my office, in reality the spare bedroom, pull out a sheet of paper and a pen and draft a reply.

I keep it short and cheerful with a hint of surprise, accepting their unexpected invitation. As I write the return address, it dawns on me that they must have moved; somewhere expensive by the look of the Thameside location. Keith is obviously doing very well.

Ali meets me at the station in Avignon. I'd decided to take the Eurostar rather than fly; all that hassle getting to Heathrow, the security, the hanging around – it was so much easier to nip across town to the terminal at Waterloo, book a first-class seat and sit back to enjoy the French countryside speeding by. I even managed to practise my schoolboy French with a charming couple who boarded the train in Paris.

I spot her immediately when I exit the station. Still the same Ali, slim figure, straight dark hair – even the huge sunglasses can't disguise her. She'd seen the train arrive and was waiting by the entrance. I hurry over to give her a big hug and she kisses me on both cheeks. 'It's so good to see you, Marcus. I'm so pleased you decided to come.' She takes my hand and steers me in the direction of the car park. I'm impressed by the bright red convertible Golf GTI with French plates; she and Keith obviously spend enough time here to warrant a left-hand drive car. The roof is down so I sling my case on the back seat and climb in. 'Are you thirsty? Do you want to stop for a drink on the way?' she asks before starting the car.

'No, thanks, Ali, I'm fine. I can't wait to see this villa of yours.'

She looks at me and gives a kind of "French" shrug. 'It's all Keith's idea really. I didn't have much to do with it. He saw it advertised and decided he wanted it; said it would be perfect for family holidays and entertaining. To be honest, I think he prefers the entertaining to the holidays.' She gives a little laugh as she accelerates past an ancient 2CV and speeds off down the empty road.

The villa sits on a ridge overlooking the tiny village of Suzette. I learn later that the jagged hills behind the villa are the Dentelles and form the northernmost boundary of Provence. The house itself is a converted farmhouse; typically Provençal in style with rendered walls the colour of honey and faded blue shutters at every window.

Ali fusses around getting me settled in my room then pulls me by the hand to the kitchen, opening the fridge and pouring two generous glasses of white wine. 'Come on,' she says, 'I'll give you a quick tour.'

It's clear that a lot of money has been spent on what was once a basic rural dwelling. There seem to be enough bedrooms and bathrooms to cater for at least ten guests. 'Out there,' says Ali, pointing through a bedroom window, 'we've converted one of the barns to a self-contained flat. The kids love it there, if and when they decide to come.' She continues downstairs, guiding me through the dining room, a huge sitting room, the TV room with a massive wall-mounted screen, Keith's office ('out of bounds,' she jokes) and back to the kitchen, about the size you'd expect to find in a well-equipped restaurant. Our tour continues outside where I take in the naturally shaded area with plush seating for barbecues, the immaculate gardens, the tennis court, the grove of citrus and olive trees; it all looks very picture-book Provençal. If I was being truthful, I'd have to say the ultra-modern infinity pool, all glass and concrete, seems a bit out of place, but it commands an amazing view across the valley below. If you could choose the perfect villa to put in an estate agent's brochure, this would be it.

'Wow! Ali, it's amazing! You must love being here.'

She takes a sip of wine and gives me a kind of embarrassed smile. 'It is rather lovely, isn't it?'

'So, where is everyone?' I ask, looking around, taking in the empty garden and quiet house.

'Well, Keith's taken his guests on a wine-buying trip. This is Côtes du Rhône country – you probably knew that – so they're doing a tour of the vineyards. I'm expecting them back for supper. Sophie and Jake have gone for a bike ride with their friends, so I guess they'll be back when they need feeding again.'

'How old are the kids now?' I ask.

'Sophie's twenty-six and Jake's two years younger.'

'And they still come on holiday with Mummy and Daddy?'

'Only when Mummy and Daddy are paying.' She laughs. 'It's what kids do these days.'

Suddenly she slaps her forehead. 'Oh my God! How rude of me. Here I am talking about food and I haven't even asked if you're hungry. You must be starving!' She heads off back to the house and I follow her along the path, brushing my hand through the lavender border, releasing the undeniable aroma of Provence.

Over a plate of cheese and a simple salad, and another glass of excellent wine, we exchange our most recent news about the places we've been and the people we've seen. It's strange, but apart from the other members of the band, there's very little overlap amongst the people we know or the circles we move in. After half an hour, it becomes obvious we've run out of current news. Ali picks up the empty plates. 'You must be feeling a bit tired. Why don't you go and sort yourself out and we'll go for a swim later. I need to start preparing our supper. If it was up to me, we'd have something really easy, but Keith likes to put on a bit of a show for his guests, so I'd better get weaving.' She looks at me and nods her head towards the stairs. 'Go on, come down about four.'

Upstairs, I unpack my bag and put away my clothes in the large *armoire* that stands against one wall, a small sachet of dried lavender nestling in each of its drawers. The bathroom is en suite, so I decide to take a shower and then lie on the bed, opening up the latest John Irving I'd started reading on the train.

The wine at lunchtime must have made me sleepy because the next thing I know there's a gentle tapping at the door and Ali's voice saying, 'Marcus, are you awake? I'm just going down to the pool. Come down if you want to.'

'Oh, hi, Ali,' I reply. 'Yeah, sure, be down in a minute.' I look at my watch. It's well past four but the sun is still bright outside. I pull on a pair of trunks, grab my Ray-Bans and the huge beach towel that Ali has thoughtfully provided and make my way to the pool.

She's already in the water, wearing a bright green bikini and concentrating on a steady breaststroke; I watch her for a while, allowing my skin to adjust to the warmth of the sun. She sees me as she turns at the end of a length. 'Come on, it's lovely! But no jumping! Use the steps.' I drop my sunglasses and the towel onto the nearest sun lounger and step into the pool. The water is surprisingly cold and it takes a moment or two before I can pluck up the courage to launch myself towards her, treading water in the middle of the pool. 'Isn't this great? I love this time of day. Aren't you glad you came?'

I nod and smile in agreement. 'It's fantastic, Ali, really lovely.'

We swim side by side for a few lengths without speaking then Ali heads to the steps and pulls herself out of the pool, holding onto the steel handrail. I watch her pick up a towel, standing while she raises her arms to pat her hair dry. I realise it's the first time I've seen her in a bikini since we were on the beach in Cunit; it must be, what, over thirty years ago? She doesn't look like the shy, skinny young girl she was at eighteen. She's kept her slim figure, but now there's a toned firmness that makes me think she must be spending time at the gym. In my idle observations on beaches in various locations, I've come to the conclusion that a woman who looks stunning, in an obvious way, all tight curves and groomed to a degree that would require high maintenance, can often look surprisingly unattractive when wearing a swimsuit; on the other hand, a less glamorous woman who's not trying to draw attention to herself can often reveal a stunning beach body. Ali fits into the second category by a mile, not that, to my eyes, anyone could ever describe her as anything but beautiful.

I carry on doing a few lengths then turn onto my back, floating and enjoying the feeling of the sun on my face.

'Do you want a beer, Marcus?' she calls out. I raise my arm out of the water and give her a thumbs-up. By the time I've pulled myself out of the pool and dried myself, two bottles have appeared on the low table that sits between the loungers. 'Cheers!' says Ali and clinks her bottle to mine. 'Here's to sunny times!'

'I'll drink to that,' I say, and we clink our bottles again.

Our doze by the pool is interrupted by the sound of a car noisily crunching up the driveway, followed by the typically loud voices of English people on holiday who have enjoyed a good lunch. I look up to see Keith advancing towards the pool followed by two couples. 'Marco! You old bugger, you made it!' I just manage to stand up before he engulfs me in a bear-like man hug.

'Come and meet these lovely people, they're dying to meet one of my old band mates!' He's obviously been playing the "I used to be in a band" card again. I assume the proper, slightly embarrassed look while shaking hands. He tells me their names, which I forget instantly. Two identical-looking men with their identical-looking wives, all slightly the worse for wear. 'Ali,' he booms in her direction, 'we've had such a cracking time; bought loads of wine and had a great meal at Chez wots-his-name.'

'I hope you haven't been drinking and driving,' says Ali. 'You know what the French police are like.'

'Of course not, darling, I've been a very good boy,' replies Keith, winking at one of the men.

'Well, I expect you'd all like to freshen up. Why don't we meet for drinks on the terrace around seven while I get on with supper? Marcus, you can give me a hand if you wouldn't mind.'

Keith and the two couples amble back towards the house leaving Ali and I to resume our sun lounge.

'So, who are these people?' I ask.

'Clients,' replies Ali. 'They spend a lot of advertising money with Keith, that's why he's invited them. The slightly balding man is Clive and his wife is Claire, and the other chap is Tony and his wife's name is Jan. I'm not sure if it's short for Janet or Janice.'

'Clive and Claire?' I muse. 'They fit rather well together, don't they?'

'Don't be rude,' say Ali, giggling.

'How long are they here for?'

'They're going at the end of the week, thank goodness. They're nice enough people but I don't really like having to entertain, especially when I'm on holiday; but I suppose we wouldn't have this place if Keith didn't have clients like them.'

'Well, you're entertaining me,' I suggest.

'You're different,' she says. 'You're a friend. Anyway, I like you.'

Suddenly she sits up and looks at me over the top of her sunglasses. 'Marcus, you look awfully pale. Have you brought any suncream? It's been really hot here.' I give her a kind of hopeless shrug. 'Well, you can borrow some of ours. There's always plenty left in the house. You'd better start tomorrow, can't have you getting sunburn.'

We eat our evening meal sitting outside at the large rustic table set up under the vine-covered pergola. Ali has produced a lovely meal of pasta with a provençal sauce, a salad niçoise with garlicky bread and a tarte tatin with crème fraiche. My only contribution had been to set the table and light the candles. Ali's kids and their friends appear long enough to load up their plates and head back to the barn. Keith is in his element, encouraging everyone to sample the wines he bought, giving us his views on each bottle he opens. I have to smile at the way he coaxes everyone into the conversation, the way he flatters and cajoles, how he charms the wives of Clive and Tony – it's no wonder he's so bloody successful. I'm sitting between Jan and Claire who seem to have worn off the effects of their indulgent lunch. They're both fully made-up and wearing brightly coloured cocktail dresses, with tanned shoulders and cleavage very much to the fore. As the new man in the group, I seem to be attracting a lot of their attention. And, as the wine flows, they become more friendly, asking questions and gently flirting; Claire stroking my arm on one side and Jan smoothing my thigh on the other. I answer their questions politely, smiling at each in turn, knowing it's all just part of the game. In different circumstances, I might have suggested to one or the other a clandestine meeting later that evening; after all, a shag is a shag. But tonight, for some reason, I only have eyes for Ali as she fusses around the table being the perfect hostess.

By now, the conversation has moved on to Keith's vast collection of cognacs and local *marcs*, and I can feel the long day's travel, and the wine, beginning to catch up on me. I decide to make my excuses and retire to bed, much to the teasing disappointment of the two women and the mocking cries of 'lightweight' from Keith. On my way through the kitchen, I catch up with Ali loading the dishwater. I take a bottle of cold water from the fridge and give her a goodnight kiss on each cheek.

'See you in the morning,' she says, smiling.

FIFTEEN

ALISON

'How are you finding Marco?' Keith asks, refilling the drinks fridge with more beers and wine ready for another day of entertaining. 'Seems a bit quiet to me, do you think he's all right?'

'Mmm, I think so. I haven't had the chance to spend much time with him since he arrived. You and your guests have rather monopolised him. When are they going, by the way?'

'*Our* guests, darling, don't forget. I know it's a lot of work for you, but they really do appreciate it and so do I. As a matter of fact, I'm driving them to the airport tomorrow, then we can have a few days on our own with the kids. Promise.'

'What about Marcus?'

'Oh, he can stay. He's more like family.'

The young ones haven't put in an appearance so far. I can't blame them catching up on sleep, they're all working so hard climbing the ladders of their chosen professions. Apart from Jake, that is, working for his father, although I'm pretty sure Keith keeps his son's nose well and truly to the grindstone. Poor Jake, I'm not entirely convinced he's cut out to be an entrepreneur. He's more of a dreamer, like me.

I wave to the guests as I walk past the tennis court. Keith is umpiring a game of mixed doubles and dispensing refreshments at the same time. He sees me and waves back. 'If you see Marco, tell him we need him here,' he shouts, 'and you too, we need another couple!'

I find Marcus by the pool, lying in the shade of an umbrella, reading his book.

'Hey, how are you? Are you okay?'

'Yeah, fine, thanks.' He smiles.

'Keith's worried you've been a bit quiet.'

'No, I really am fine, honest. Just enjoying this wonderful peace and quiet.'

'And keeping out of the way of Jan and Claire,' I tease.

'They are a bit OTT, aren't they? Don't you think their husbands notice?'

'I'm sure they don't care. Anyway, I thought you'd be used to being a magnet for bored housewives, a single man like you.'

He looks up at me. 'Yeah, well, not anymore. I think those days might be over.' It's difficult to tell if he's sad or relieved.

'Come on,' I say, holding out a hand, 'Keith wants us to join in the tennis. We can play the winners. Besides, they're going home tomorrow, then we can all relax!'

After the tennis, where Marcus and I show sufficient latent skills to emerge as eventual winners, complete with kisses all round and a bottle of champagne – opened with a flourish by Keith – we all leap into the pool. For the first time in days, I feel at ease, not having to be the "hostess". It was no longer "clients" or "guests", just people on holiday having a good time; splashing, laughing, enjoying the sun. By the time the kids arrive, planning to start their day with a reviving swim, an energetic game of volleyball is underway, women versus the men, with much cheating and deliberate foul play. The young ones look on with horror at the "grown-ups" having fun and decide to retire to the house in search of food.

As we lay in the sun, drying off, Keith announces he has booked a table for everyone for supper at the local bistro. He'd told me his plan when he was getting dressed this morning. I'd breathed a silent sigh of relief at not having to prepare another evening meal. 'That's a lovely idea,' I said. 'I hope your clients appreciate all you've been doing for them, they've been thoroughly spoilt.'

He shrugged. 'Just as long as they keep spending their money with me.' The look on his face told me that as much as he might conjure up entertaining fun and games, it was still all about business for him.

The departing couples are up early the next morning ready for the journey to Avignon to catch their flight back to London. By the time everyone's had breakfast and loaded up the car, it's nearly 10am. Marcus and I wave after them as Keith accelerates down the driveway in his Range Rover, leaving a cloud of pale dust to settle. I make a fresh cafetière while Marcus loads the dishwasher, then we wander down to the pool, taking our coffee with us.

The day is already hot, so we lie on the sun loungers in the shade, sipping our coffee. There's something I've been wanting to ask Marcus.

'So,' I begin, 'I was a bit surprised when you said you were coming on your own. The last I heard you had a lady friend; for quite a while, I gather.'

Marcus puts down his cup. 'Yeah, well, "had" is the operative word there, Ali.'

'How long were you together?'

'Nearly two years.'

'Wow! That must be a record for you, Marcus.'

He smiles but looks quite sad.

'So, what happened? Did she want more from the relationship?'

'No,' he replies, 'believe it or not, it was the other way around.'

I don't say anything. I sense he wants to say more so I wait for him to continue.

'Strange really, when you think about it. I know I've done my fair share of dumping girlfriends in the past, but I really thought she was "the one". We were having such a good time, she looked amazing, the sex was great, and then "bang". It was over, right out of the blue.'

'So, how did it end? Did she say why?'

'Well, the timing wasn't great, the day after my birthday. She suddenly blurted out that it "wasn't working for her". She felt "tied down", that she was more of a "free spirit", whatever the fuck that means.'

'Oh, Marcus, I'm so sorry.' I don't think I've ever seen him looking so downcast. 'Had she been married before? Did she have children?'

'I think that was a large part of the problem. She'd never been married but had two kids from different fathers, plus she still had a job and a child at school. She told me she didn't have the energy for a relationship. In fairness, I think she realised I had strong feelings for her and she didn't want to be responsible for those feelings, so she backed away.'

'I think you're being too kind,' I say. 'Sounds to me more like she had a problem with relationships.'

'Yeah, you're probably right, although I guess some people might call it karma, being the one to get dumped.' He looks over and gives me a rueful smile as if to show me he's getting over it. We don't say anything for a while then he seems to perk up, more like the "old" Marcus.

'So that's why you've got me all to yourself, darling!' He laughs and claps his hands. 'Come on, let's swim.'

Keith gets back at lunchtime. He looks exhausted. I've seen him like this before; he puts so much energy into making sure people are having a good time that when it stops, he looks deflated, older too. I worry sometimes what effect all this entertaining is having on his health, but when I mention anything he just laughs and tells me he's "perfectly fit". It doesn't stop him taking to his bed for the afternoon. Sophie and Jake are out with their friends so I suggest to Marcus we take my car and go exploring. I've heard there's a good *brocante* market in Carpentras and I want to see if I can find something interesting for the house.

By the time we set off, Marcus seems to have recovered his usual relaxed self. He fills me in with stories of what he's been up to since we last saw him. He doesn't say much about his time with the girlfriend. I sense it's still a bit raw for him to talk about, so I don't pursue it. He seems to lead such an exciting life – exhibitions, openings, book launches, parties – keeping up his connections in the music and TV worlds; it makes my life sound quite dull by comparison. I'm laughing as I drive, listening to the scandalous gossip he's regaling me with about the celebrities he's met, although I'm sure he's embellishing some of the tales for my benefit. I can't help teasing him when he tells me he plays golf. 'Not very rock "n" roll,' I say, but he explains it's a good way to keep in touch with his old rugby pals.

When I ask him if he's ever played at Keith's club in Berkshire, he laughs. 'Have you any idea how much the fees are?' I have to confess I don't; it's a part of Keith's life he keeps to himself.

By the time we arrive at the market, some of the stalls are packing up already. I should have remembered that these local events start early. No matter; we breeze around various stalls picking up items here and there. Eventually, I find a couple of wicker baskets I take a fancy to and an old map of Provence. Meanwhile, Marcus has found a straw hat. He puts it on and asks me what I think. 'It looks great,' I say, 'all you need now is a cream linen suit and you'll look like a proper Edwardian gent on holiday.' He laughs and bows and pays the man the money.

'Come on,' he says, 'enough shopping. Let's go and find a drink,' and he takes my arm and steers me away from any more purchases.

While we wait for the drinks to arrive, a *pression* for Marcus, a *monaco* for me, I look at him as he adjusts his new hat. He must be over fifty now, but he's still a very good-looking man; he has the relaxed manner of someone who is at ease with the world. Or maybe that's just an image he projects. After all, as I recall, he did use to work in advertising.

The waiter exits the bar, tray in hand, and brings over our drinks. We clink our glasses together. 'Cheers,' we say, content to sit for a while and watch the world go by.

Suddenly Marcus stands up. 'Back in a jiffy,' he says and wanders off down the street. He returns in less than five minutes, sits down and begins to unwrap a packet of cigarettes.

'Marcus!' I say, in mock horror, 'I didn't know you still smoked!' He's already struck a match and inhaled deeply.

'I don't, really. I just couldn't resist the idea of a Gitanes.

I used to smoke them all the time. There's something about the sunshine, the smell of the street, sitting outdoors drinking a French beer – it just seemed like the perfect moment. Want one?' He offers me the pack; I'm tempted but decline. He's already stubbing out the cigarette. 'Actually, not sure if that was a great idea,' says Marcus. 'I love the smell, but I'd forgotten what they taste like. Maybe I'll just sniff the packet.' Marcus orders another *demi* and looks towards me. 'So, Ali, tell me about you. What have you been up to? What's it like being married to a millionaire?'

I know he's teasing but I can't help being slightly defensive. 'What do you want to know? About me or the millionaire part?'

'Sorry, Ali,' he says. 'I wasn't being nosy. About you, of course.'

'Not a lot to tell, really. Bringing up the children, looking after Keith, sorting out my parents' stuff after they died, keeping two homes going. All the usual stuff.' It sounds very mundane when I say it like that.

'And how about Keith, how's he doing?'

'Oh, you know Keith, still totally driven, one deal after another. Now he's got a mobile he's always on the phone – in the car, in the restaurant, on holiday. It's even next to the bed! I sometimes wonder if he's happy with me holding the fort at home or if he'd prefer someone, you know, a bit more glamorous, a bit more extrovert.'

'Don't put yourself down, Ali. I'm sure he really appreciates you, and you still look amazing. You've hardly changed since we went to Cunit.' I smile and thank him. I didn't think he even noticed me in Spain! 'Aren't you still involved in your music? You were always the most talented of all of us.'

Gosh, I think to myself, *that's two compliments on the trot!* 'Well, I used to do a lot of session work but after I had the children, it just became too hard. Late nights, short notice – it was too much to juggle and eventually they stopped asking.'

'So, you don't play at all?'

'Very occasionally. There's a piano at the house but I've hardly touched it.'

Marcus leans forward and strokes my hand. 'Well, I hope you'll play for me while I'm here. I'd really like that.'

I smile at him. 'Maybe,' I say.

It's early evening by the time Marcus and I get back to the villa, and Keith is up and about. He's wandering around in the kitchen opening cupboards and looking in the fridge. 'Have we got anything to eat, darling? I'm starving.' We'd stopped at the supermarket on the way back from Carpentras and I dump the bags on the table.

'Here we are, no need to panic. Why don't you pour us all a drink and go and light the barbecue? I'll give you a shout when I'm ready.'

The young folk decide they will eat with us tonight. It's been their last day at Suzette and they're due to catch the TGV in the morning. The wine flows, Keith's happy cooking sausages and steaks, and Marcus is engaging in conversation with Sophie and Jake and their friends. He seems to know an awful lot about the bands they like; I'm quite impressed. I must admit I stopped listening to their music several years ago. Even if I'm not playing anymore, I'd rather listen to the classical tunes in my head. Everyone agrees an early night would be a good idea. I excuse Sophie and Jake from doing the dishes (not that they ever offer, although their friends, out of politeness, do) and send them off to pack, knowing the morning is likely to be fraught.

The morning turns out to be more complicated than I expected. Keith's been on the phone since 8am talking to his office. He says he needs to go back and sort out some business, so instead of us going back by car he'll take the train with Sophie and Jake.

'Do you really have to? Is it that important?' I'd asked as he came out of the shower. I was feeling rather abandoned. 'What am I supposed to do with Marcus?'

'I'm sorry, darling, it'll only be for a couple of days, three, tops. The train will be quicker than driving and when I get back we can have that slow drive home through France we always talked about. Besides, I'm sure you and Marcus can find plenty to do. It was *your* idea to invite him after all.'

Keith decides to drive everyone to the station and leave the car for when he gets back. Within an hour, they're all packed and gone, hugs and kisses all round, leaving Marcus and me in the kitchen to finish a late breakfast.

'I'm sorry, Marcus, it all seems a bit rude, everyone disappearing like that. I hope you don't mind.'

'Don't be silly, Ali. I'm sure Keith wouldn't have left if it wasn't necessary. Got to keep the wheels of the media empire going, you know!'

'Mmm, I'm not so sure,' I say.

'What do you mean?'

I hesitate for a moment, wondering if I should tell Marcus what's been on my mind. 'I think Keith's having an affair.'

'What, Keith!' He makes it sound like it's the most ridiculous thing he's ever heard. 'Are you sure? Who with?'

'His PA, for Christ's sake!' I stand up and take my breakfast things over to the sink, breaking a cup in the process. 'What a bloody cliché.' I grip the edge of the sink and feel the tears begin to run down my cheek. I sense Marcus standing behind me, hesitating, not quite knowing what to say or do. Then he puts his hand on my arm and I turn around and bury my head into his shoulder.

'Oh, Ali, I'm so sorry,' says Marcus, stroking my back. 'How did you find out?'

'Just little things. Late nights at the office, vague arrangements for meetings, taking more interest in what he's wearing. Then I found a restaurant receipt in one of his jackets I was taking to the cleaners. It was for an evening with me he'd cancelled. God knows, Keith's no oil painting. It's not like he's the most attractive man on the planet! (Nor the greatest lover in the world, I wanted to say.) Like I said, maybe he wants someone younger, more glamorous.'

'Don't be daft,' says Marcus. 'It's more likely she's attracted to his money. Have you met her?'

'A couple of times, all make-up, glossy hair and tight sweater, the classic secretary. "Oh, hullo, Mrs Fairfax, how lovely to see you. Your husband is on a call, but I'll let him know you're here." You know the type.'

Marcus smiles and rather sweetly offers me a sheet of kitchen roll to wipe my nose. 'But do you know if they're actually, you know, doing it?'

I laugh. 'Well if you're asking have I caught them at it, no, of course not! I'm not spying on them!'

'So, have you said anything to him?'

'No. I keep meaning to and then the moment passes. I suppose I'm not sure what the outcome would be.'

'Are you thinking about divorce?'

I start to pick up the pieces of the broken cup. 'Oh, I don't know, Marcus, it's all so muddled. We've been married nearly thirty years. I have a lovely life most of the time, all of this,' I say, gesturing around the room. 'Maybe it's a one-off and he'll get over it; typical mid-life crisis.'

Marcus folds his arms. 'Do you still love him?'

I smile at him. 'How does that song go? *What's Love Got to Do With It?* I honestly don't know, maybe we've both changed.'

I decide we've had enough of talking about me. 'Come on, let's go for a swim and then I'll let you take me to lunch. That's sure to cheer me up.'

Marcus kindly offers to drive. I think he feels I need a couple of drinks to help me get over my outburst this morning. We end up at a quaint bistro tucked away down a country lane. We wouldn't have found it if we hadn't seen a faded signpost by the side of the road and decided to check it out. It turns out to be perfect. We find a small table on a shaded terrace next to a slow-moving river. Marcus orders a bottle of chilled rosé and a large plate of charcuterie to share. I'm on my second glass when Marcus asks me if I've heard anything from Steve. 'No, not really,' I reply. 'I haven't heard anything for ages. Have you?'

'No, not for some time. I guess since Gloria's career took off they don't spend so much time in Spain. I often wonder what Cunit must look like now. I wonder if the Bar Estudio is still there.' Have you ever been back?' The mention of Cunit takes me back to when the band played there, when I thought Marcus might show some interest in me instead of that Swiss girl he got off with.

'I've only been to see them once, when their children were younger. It was all a bit chaotic. Gloria was getting ready to go on tour again and Steve spent most of the time in the studio he'd built. I felt more like the au pair! We ended up having an argument and we haven't spoken much since. It was all a bit silly really. I can't even remember what it was about.'

'Did you find the bar?'

'Funny you should mention that. I did look for it and discovered it had been turned into a baker's shop; no sign of it ever being a bar, quite sad really.' We spend the rest of lunchtime reminiscing about the band's trip to Spain and then start remembering some of the other gigs we played before the band broke up. We laugh about our *I Got You, Babe* duet and how we dreaded some of the venues where there was no stage – we always played better when there was some height between us and the audience. By the time the waitress brings the bill, I've drunk most of the wine and I'm beginning to feel sleepy.

Marcus settles up and steers me back gently towards the car and I'm asleep long before we get back to the villa.

SIXTEEN

MARCUS

I'm woken up by the touch of a hand sliding across my stomach. I feel a body, naked, pushing against mine.

'Ali?' my voice, sleepy, 'is that...?'

'Shhh,' she whispers, 'don't say a word.' She continues to stroke my skin and I can feel myself becoming aroused. I turn to face her. The room is almost pitch-black, but I can just make out her face, eyes open, a half-smile on her lips.

'Are you sure...?' I begin but she lifts her head and stops me with a kiss.

'I said, no talking.' She smiles and pulls me towards her. We begin to kiss with more passion, bodies moving against each other, hands exploring. I forget this is Keith's wife, the guy for whom I was best man. Instead, I'm thinking of Alison by the pool, of the teenage girl on a beach in Cunit, of the woman who clung to me in the kitchen. And I realise this is something I've thought about for a long time. I try to move myself on top, but she pushes me away and straddles me instead. We find a smooth rhythm, no words, just intakes of breath and gasps of satisfaction.

I glance up at her face, curtained by her hair, and see a look, less like pleasure, more like a determined concentration, as if she has a destination in mind. We move faster, with more urgency, and when we reach a climax together, which, in my book, is a rare experience, we stay locked together for long moments, until she collapses onto my chest and we lie there, holding each other tightly for what seems like ages.

I hesitate to break the silence. 'Are you okay?' As much as I'm amazed at what just happened, I can't get rid of the thought that this was some kind of revenge for Keith's affair or, even worse, that she was feeling sorry for me.

'Mmm, I'm fine,' she muffles into my neck. 'Thank you, that was just perfect.'

Within seconds, she's asleep.

The same thing happens the next night and the night after. And then Keith returns from his trip to London and we resume the holiday as if nothing happened. No shared glances, no furtive touching, just three middle-aged people sharing time together.

It feels weird, like I'm stuck in a *ménage à trois*: Alison's told me her suspicions about Keith and now she's slept with me.

And Keith has no idea what's going on.

Another day passes. Keith and Alison are making plans for their slow drive home through France, so I decide it's time for me to head back too. In the morning, Keith offers to drive me to Avignon to catch the train. I hug Alison in the driveway and she kisses me on both cheeks. 'Thank you for coming, Marcus, it was lovely to see you here. You take good care.' I smile back. I can see there is a deeper message in her eyes. Is it fondness or regret?

'Thanks for having me,' I say, kissing her lightly on the lips. 'It's been a real pleasure.' Then I climb into Keith's 4x4 and we're gone, in another cloud of dust.

SEVENTEEN

2005 – DAVE

The letter from the hospital arrived two weeks after my visit to my GP. They want me to come in for a biopsy. Apparently, my psa level is higher than it should be, so the next stage would be to take some samples from my prostate gland.

This all happened quite by chance. I'd been to visit an old friend in hospital who was having a knee replacement and at the last minute they couldn't operate because he had MRSA. It turns out this is not at all uncommon in hospitals, something I find rather ironic. You'd think they'd be the most hygienic of places, not somewhere you stand a good chance of catching a disease.

So, I decided to go to the doc's to see if I'd caught it as well.

While I was there, getting my nose swabbed, the doctor asked me when was the last time I'd had my psa checked. As I couldn't remember when, or if at all, he suggested he take a blood sample. 'A reasonable precaution for a gentleman of your age,' was how he put it. A few days later, the result showed my level was at the "concerned" stage, so my doctor asked me to give another sample. When this one came back with the same result, he thought I'd better have the biopsy. Hence the letter from the hospital.

By this point, I'd already Googled "prostate cancer", so I had a fair idea of what the process might be, although I hadn't mentioned it to anyone else. Who was I going to tell anyway? Apart from Marcus, I had very few of what I would call close friends, and I didn't really want to bother him. Besides, until I got the results of the biopsy, there wasn't a lot to tell.

With the letter was a leaflet explaining the procedure. It said that some men might find it "painful" but usually there might only be some "discomfort". It made me wonder what my own pain threshold might be, something I hadn't had to test up till now.

As it turned out, I needn't have been concerned. Claire, the clinical nurse in charge, was very gentle, or so it felt, and kept up a steady flow of light conversation as she inserted a sequence of needles into my bottom. 'There,' she said after what felt like twenty minutes of probing, 'all done, David. You'll get a letter in the next few days for an appointment with the consultant, who will give you the results. You might get a bit of bleeding tonight but that's quite normal, so nothing to worry about,' she added, cheerfully.

Ten days later, I'm talking to the consultant, a surgeon. 'Call me Liz,' she suggests when I tell her I understand her male colleagues are addressed as "Mr", but I don't how to address a lady surgeon. Liz explains that the biopsy indicated there are sufficient levels of cancer cells in my prostate to consider various treatment options. These include hormone treatment, radiotherapy and surgery, each with its own advantages and disadvantages. My searches on the internet had already given some of the information I needed, so I asked her what she would do if it was her. Obviously, not her exactly, but any male whom she might know well. She stroked her tummy in an absent-minded way. Up to that point, I hadn't noticed she was pregnant. 'Well, it if was my husband and he presented with the same results as you, I would recommend surgery.'

'And you would be doing the operation?' I had a sudden vision of her unborn child kicking at precisely the moment she had the scalpel in her hand, with me getting more removed than I'd bargained for. My voice must have conveyed my concern.

'Don't worry, David, we use robotic surgery here. I've got the controls, but the robot does the surgery. It's very accurate, we do ten of these a week.'

'Okay,' I say, sounding a lot more confident than I'm feeling. 'Let's do it.' Liz assures me I would only need to be in hospital for one day, but she doesn't recommend driving. She asks if there's anyone can come and fetch me and take me home. 'Well, I live alone,' I explain, 'but I'm sure I can think of someone.'

The only person I can think of, of course, is Marcus. When, eventually, I phoned to give him the news, there was a pause while he processed the information. Knowing him as I do, he was probably searching for the right balance between sounding shocked and concerned while at the same time trying to be upbeat and confident.

'Oh, mate,' he says, 'I'm really sorry to hear that. How long have you known? Why didn't you say anything before?' I explained that there was nothing I wanted to say until I knew for sure, and would he mind coming to collect me from the hospital on the day? 'Of course, Dave, no problem. You just tell me when and where. Maybe you should come and stay here for a while.' I said thanks but told him I hoped that wouldn't be necessary.

Four weeks later, I'm in the pre-op room at seven-thirty in the morning. This time, Liz strikes me as being rather more business-like.

She told me about some of the risks connected to the operation and I began to wonder if I'd made the right decision. She said they may have to inject my spine and I might wake up feeling my legs are "paralysed". Or, possibly, some of my nerves may get cut during the operation, leaving me with a colostomy bag, 'temporarily but unlikely.' Then I was asked to sign a form to say I understood the risks. By this stage, my confidence was beginning to evaporate rapidly, but it was too late to back out.

Within minutes, I was wheeled to the operating theatre. Then something was injected into my hand and I remember counting backwards, and the next thing I knew I heard a voice saying, 'Wake up, David,' and the nurse telling me it's four hours later.

Liz was right about my legs. I could feel them with my hands, but I couldn't move them. I experienced a wave of panic. Then I searched to feel around my waist. As far as I could tell, there was no tube coming out of me. *So, no colostomy bag,* I thought. The relief of this discovery counteracted the concern I had about my paralysed legs. The next thing I knew I was being taken to the recovery ward.

So, here I am, still feeling very drowsy. Every few minutes, I try to send a message from my brain to move my legs but nothing's happening. I try and raise myself to have a look down the bed, but I don't have the energy to lift the dead weight of my legs. A nurse comes over and gives me a drink of water from a cup with a bent straw. 'How are you feeling, David?' It strikes me that everyone in the NHS seems to be on first-name terms with the patients. I try and respond with a nod of the head and a smile, but it must have looked more like a grimace. 'Don't worry, you're doing really well. I'll come back later. You might be feeling hungry by then.'

I lie back on the pillow and send another message to my legs; still nothing happening. However, I do make one discovery. I can feel a tube coming out of my penis. When I twist my head to one side, I can see the tube appearing from beneath the sheet and disappearing into a plastic bag attached to the side of the bed. The bag contains a yellow liquid – my piss. *That'll be the catheter they told me about*, I think, with blinding obviousness. The tube must be going straight into my bladder because I felt no sensation of needing to pee. I have the ludicrous thought that this must be what it was like to be a baby, just letting go without the need to hold on. In a strange way, quite satisfying.

I lie here and let my mind wander. I'm trying to remember the last time I was in a hospital, as a patient not a visitor. I recall a couple of dental treatments for root canal work and a private appointment to remove a cyst. Suddenly the episode of a bizarre head injury comes to mind. I was on my way back to London from a meeting in Milton Keynes when I had the idea to visit the church where I knew some of my relatives were buried. The family used to own the farm next door and I had distant memories of visiting for Sunday afternoon tea when my parents bought their first car, a Ford Consul, a blue one. I can see it now.

I parked outside the church. A traditional lych-gate stood at the entrance with a grassy bank on either side where the original hedge had been removed. I decided to run up the bank instead of bothering with the gate. The next thing I knew, I felt an enormous bang on the head and

I'm lying on the ground. John, the colleague travelling with me, who up to this point hadn't shown much interest in my side trip to the church, jumped out of the car. In my haste to reach the path, I must have misjudged the angle of the slope between the bank and the roof over the gate, and my head had crunched into a thick timber beam.

'Are you all right?' he asked.

It seemed pretty clear I wasn't all right; otherwise, I wouldn't be lying there on the grass, but I let it go. 'Yes, I think so,' I mumbled, feeling my head rather gingerly.

A lump was already beginning to form, and blood and hair were stuck to my fingers. By now, I was trying to stand up. John gave me a hand while inspecting my head. 'That doesn't look good,' he said, 'I think we need to get to a hospital.'

'No, I'm sure I'll be fine,' I said, waving him away, trying not to make a fuss.

'You can't see what I can, David,' he replied, sounding rather too serious for my liking.

He steered me towards the passenger seat, strapped me in, then got behind the wheel and headed for the nearest hospital. It was in Luton, of all places, where, after a three-hour wait, I had fourteen stitches in my scalp, an anti-tetanus jab and a handful of painkillers.

So much for my quest for knowledge. I never did find out which of my relatives were buried in that church.

I send another message to my legs. This time, I detect a response in my left foot. I try flexing it a couple of times, making a small circle under the sheet. You can't imagine the relief that flooded through me. *Jesus*, I thought, *I'm not paralysed!* I know that might sound pathetic but when you haven't been able to move anything from the waist down for more than three hours you begin to fear the worst. I'd already been working out in my mind how I might use my drum kit if I couldn't move my feet. Maybe some kind of attachment to my knees or elbows? I haven't told Marcus I've started drumming again. I joined a "retro" band recently, the kind that plays nostalgic music from the forties and fifties. The music's not exactly my preferred choice and I'm really not keen on wearing the mock uniform – they've got me dressed up as a private in the army – so I'm pretty sure Marcus would find the whole thing very amusing. He would probably put "forties nostalgia" somewhere slightly above "sea shanties" in his list of music to avoid. Still, it keeps my hand in and gets me out of the house, as they say, so no bad thing really.

The effect of the anaesthetic is gradually beginning to wear off and soon I'm able to move both feet and raise one leg. I'm also beginning to feel hungry; I haven't eaten since the night before.

Right on cue, the nurse returns with a sandwich and drink. I chew slowly on a tasteless combination of cheese and tomato while she pulls up a chair and explains how to deal with the catheter; how to attach it to my leg, how to empty it and how not to get it wet when I have a shower. 'Are you okay?' she asks, noticing that I've stopped eating.

'No, not really, I think I'm going to be sick.' A pre-formed bowl, made of the same material as egg boxes, swiftly appears under my chin.

'Here, use this,' says the nurse. 'It's just the anaesthetic. You'll feel better afterwards.' I gag a couple of times but don't puke. The remedy seems to be to leave the sandwich to one side, unfinished.

Another couple of hours have passed and the nurse has returned to encourage me to get out of bed. She gives me her arm to steady myself and helps me swivel my legs over the side. With a bit of a heave, I push myself up and stand, rather unsteadily, feeling a sense of utmost achievement. 'That's good, David.' She sounds genuinely pleased. 'Now try and take a few steps. The sooner we get you walking, the sooner you'll be out of here.' I let go of her arm and walk slowly to the end of the bed, turn and walk back, a broad smile on my face. 'Well done,' she says. 'I'm going to speak to the doctor now and he'll let me know if you're good to go.' She detaches the catheter bag from the bed and straps it to my leg. 'Why don't you try getting dressed? I'll be back as soon as I can.'

I sit on the edge of the bed and rummage around in the plastic bag the hospital provided for the clothes I arrived in. Fortunately, I'd worn an old pair of jogging pants to the hospital –worn once in an ill-judged attempt to get fit – thinking they might be more suitable for "outdoor wear" than pyjamas. The leg was wide enough to allow me to fit one limb inside with the bag attached. Pulling up the joggers, the elasticated waistband fitting snugly over my stomach, I finish getting dressed and lower myself into the bedside chair. It feels slightly uncomfortable knowing I haven't been able to return my underpants to their usual location.

I'm absorbed in my book, the latest Wally Lamb, when my friendly nurse comes towards me. 'Right, David.' She smiles. 'I've spoken to the doctor and he reckons you're okay to go home. Is there someone collecting you?' I tell her a friend is going to fetch me.

'Make sure they know which ward you're on or they'll be looking for ages in this place.' She gives me a leaflet and explains that I'll need to contact the hospital again to have the catheter removed. 'It's all in the leaflet. Good luck!' And with that, she's off in the direction of another patient.

I call Marcus on my mobile. 'Hey, mate,' he says in a cheerful voice, 'I've been waiting for your call. How's it going?' I tell him I'm ready to be collected, if that's still okay? 'Of course it is. I'm on my way. Should be there in less than an hour.' True to his word, he arrives on time. I see his welcome face smiling as he walks down the ward. 'Okay, let's go,' he says, picking up my overnight bag. 'Nice trousers, by the way!'

We walk out of the hospital and into the car park; Marcus slowly, me rather gingerly, feeling the weight of the bag strapped to my leg. The thought crosses my mind I've been in hospital less than twelve hours and yet I've had a major operation.

That really is amazing.

EIGHTEEN

2000 – KEITH

'Alison's been behaving strangely ever since we came back from France.' Sylvia has just been asking me how "things" are at home. She turns her head to check the clock on the bedside table.

'What do you mean?'

'More distant than usual. She's always been a bit vague, a bit distracted. I've tended to put it down to her creative temperament. She often looks as if she's composing something in her head, but just lately she looks disinterested, just drifting about, as if she's bored being at home.'

'Well, that doesn't sound like someone who is behaving strangely.' Sylvia slides closer to me and strokes my chest. 'Maybe she *is* bored. Perhaps she needs to find a job or get involved with a charity or something. God! I'd be bored if I had to stay at home all day.' That's one thing I can say about Sylvia; she would laugh at the idea of being a housewife but she does make the perfect mistress. Since she took over from my last PA, she's become a real asset. I'm not stupid, I know it's not my body that attracts her; it's much more likely she enjoys having a wealthy boss. And in her world, wealth means power. But she is bloody good at her job, and having sex with me probably gives her a feeling of power too.

She moves her hand below my waist, stroking skin softly. 'Do you think she suspects anything?' The way she says it makes it sound like she's not very concerned at all.

'Jesus! I hope not, at least I don't think so. I'm sure she thinks I haven't got it in me.' By now, Sylvia has a firm grip on my penis. She smiles as she lowers her hips onto my stiff cock.

'Well, one thing's for sure,' she says, pursing her lips with pleasure, 'you've most certainly got something in me.' I look up and watch her as she leans back, closing her eyes. God! I'm a lucky bastard. Then I feel a sudden stab of guilt as the thought of Alison flashes into my mind. God, I really am being a bastard.

Sylvia slides out of bed as soon as the sex is over. 'I'm going to take a shower. You might want one too before you go.' She's completely at ease in the nude. She gives me a wink over her shoulder; she knows I'll be looking at her body. I can't help thinking she has the same improbable figure as Modesty Blaise, the cartoon strip that featured in my mother's *Daily Mirror* when I was growing up. An indelible image.

I listen to the rush of water from the shower and go over the events of the day and how I've ended up in Sylvia's bed – again.

Since returning from France, I'd been trying to put together a deal that would move a lot of my publishing business from printed material onto the internet. The country was still in the early days of web-based retailing, but I'd been feeling for some time it was going to be the direction the public would want to go. I mean, why would you want to buy a handful of newspapers and magazines when you could sit at your computer and flip through page after page without leaving home? Of course, it was going to require a big investment in technology, and I'd had to persuade some fairly sceptical people at the bank to put in the money. But we got there, eventually. Back at the office, Sylvia had helped me compose a personal email to the managers of my subsidiary companies. My own memos tended to be direct and business-like, whereas she was able to add a friendlier, warmer tone. Her choice of words was going to be necessary as some of these guys might find themselves out of a job if they couldn't adapt to the new working arrangements. Satisfied with the draft, she headed off to her office to send out the emails, leaving me to call Alison. The phone rang for a while before she picked up. 'Hi, it's me,' I said, keeping my voice neutral, 'how's your day been?'

There was a pause before she spoke. 'Oh, hi. Yes, good, thanks. Are you on your way?'

'Not quite,' I lied, 'I've got to meet a couple of guys who are only in town for a day or two. It shouldn't take long; be home about eight.'

'Okay,' she said, sounding as if she wasn't taking much notice. 'Will you have eaten something, or shall I wait?'

'No, you go ahead, don't wait for me. I'll probably grab something at the meeting. See you later, darling.'

'Yes, fine,' she said, and hung up.

Sylvia came back into my office carrying two gin and tonics.

'Here,' she said, placing a glass in front of me, 'it's been a very good day. I think you've earnt this.' I swivelled to face her as she came around to my side of the desk. As we clinked our drinks, she lowered her head and brushed my ear with her lips. 'So,' she whispered, 'shall we go back to my place?'

She knew I'd find it hard to say no.

Sylvia comes out of the bathroom wrapped in a thick robe and a towel round her head. 'I'll be in the kitchen,' she says, padding her way across the thick carpet. 'I'll make you something to eat.'

I shower and get dressed and make my way downstairs. Sylvia is sitting at the worktop in the centre of her tiny kitchen, sipping a glass of white wine. I've never asked her how she managed to acquire a mews cottage in such a fashionable part of the West End. She mentioned once she got it through "a friend of a friend", but she's never told me if she owned it or rented it; she's always struck me as being a woman of independent means. She pushes a plate towards me. 'Here, I've made you a sandwich. I heard you telling your wife you were eating out.' In all the time I've been to Sylvia's, she has never once offered to cook me a meal. Her attitude is, 'If you want home cooking then stay at home.' I'm hungry and devour the sandwich, hoping she might be able to rustle up another one. She continues skimming through the *Standard*, flicking the pages with her elegant fingers, bright red nails tapping the page, but doesn't take the hint. 'I guess you'd better get going,' she says, without looking up. I glance at my watch, it's just gone eight. If I get my foot down, I can be home by nine. 'Shouldn't take you long at this time of night.' It's uncanny how she knows what I'm thinking. She smiles and slides off the stool to give me a kiss on the cheek. 'I'll see you in the morning.' She walks me to the front door and I step out into the mews towards my parked car. As I turn to look back, she gives me a discreet wave before shutting the door firmly. The silence of the mews is broken by the rumble of the exhaust as I start the Jag. I know it may seem immature but I always get a thrill when I hear that metallic roar.

Pulling onto the driveway, I press the remote to open the garage door and park alongside Ali's Beamer. The double-width door descends behind me as I enter the house from the garage. I head towards the kitchen calling out, 'Hullo, I'm home,' but there's no answer. The kitchen is empty, but I can hear sounds coming from the TV room. I open the door and look in. Ali is lying on one of the sofas in her dressing gown, engrossed in what looks like a travel programme. 'Hi, I'm home,' I repeat, waving to her. The movement must have reflected in the screen; she turns to see me.

'Oh, hi, sorry, I didn't hear you come in.' She puts the TV on mute but doesn't turn it off. 'How did your meeting go?'

'Yeah, great, made some really good progress. Is there anything to eat?'

'I thought you said you were eating at your meeting.'

'I know, I did, but these guys were more interested in drinks than food so I decided to head home.'

'Well, there's some lasagne in the fridge that could go in the microwave. Would you like me to do it for you?'

'No, no, I can manage. You carry on with your programme.'

'Okay,' says Ali, turning back to the TV.

In the kitchen, I find the food, serve myself a large slice, shove it in the micro and pour a big glass of red while the plate rotates.

The "ping" of the machine makes me jump; my mind had wandered off thinking about Sylvia, and now I'm back home I'm beginning to feel somewhat guilty.

Ali comes into the kitchen as I'm finishing the lasagne.

'Mmm, that was delicious,' I say, pushing the empty plate away. 'You really are a great cook.' I'm trying to be complimentary, but she doesn't seem to notice, instead pouring herself another glass of wine.

'Has your programme finished? What was it about?' I'm making conversation, but she seems reluctant to engage.

'Oh, just one of those rail journey things, quite boring really, but I like the presenter.' She picks up the dirty plate, puts it in the dishwasher then sits at the table, sipping her wine.

'Ali, are you all right? You seem kind of distracted, as if your head is somewhere else.' I will come to realise that it was a mistake to start this conversation. She looks up, suddenly giving me her full attention.

'What do you mean?'

'It's hard to say, really. It's like you're disconnected from everything here, like you've got something on your mind. I've noticed you've been like it ever since we got back from France.

Is something worrying you or are you just bored?'

'I'm fine, really.' She swirls her wine around the glass and picks up an imaginary crumb with her finger.

I carry on, even though I know I'm entering dangerous territory. 'Are you sure? I mean, did anything happen at Suzette? After all, I did leave you there with Marcus and I know what kind of guy he is. Did he make a pass at you?'

'What are you suggesting? That I leapt into bed with Marcus? Don't be so fucking ridiculous!' I flinch as Ali swears; it's so unusual to hear that word coming out of her mouth.

'All I'm saying is you were there on your own. I bet he's fancied you ever since we were in the band. It really wouldn't surprise me if he tried to get you into bed.' We sit there on either side of the counter saying nothing, just staring at each other.

'Anyway, what about you?' says Ali. Here it comes; this was the territory I had unwisely stepped into.

'What do you mean, "What about you?"'

'Oh, come on, I'm not stupid. You and that secretary of yours, what's her name, Sheila? Are you telling me you're not sleeping with her?' I can see the accusation in her eyes so hold back the temptation to correct her about Sylvia's name.

'Now you're the one being fucking ridiculous! Whatever gave you that idea?'

'Because I'm not stupid, Keith.' She moves away from the counter and pours the rest of her wine down the sink. We look at each other and it's clear there is no affection between us at that moment, almost the opposite.

'I'm going to bed,' says Ali, 'you do what you like.'

I sit still and watch her walk towards the stairs. I puff out my cheeks and exhale. *Jesus*, I think to myself, *does she really know or is she guessing?* Maybe she did sleep with Marcus and that's why she's accusing me, to cover up her own behaviour. Do I really know what's going on in her life? Maybe she *is* bored and just wanted to pick a fight. I can see I'm going to have to be a lot more careful if I want to continue my relationship with Sylvia.

Relationship? Who am I kidding? She's using me as much as I'm taking advantage of her. Perhaps it *is* time to put an end to it.

The next morning, having slept in one of the guest rooms, I find Ali in the kitchen. We move about silently, fixing our own breakfasts. She puts a fresh pot of coffee on the counter between us and pours herself a mug.

'Look, Ali,' I begin, 'about last night...'

She interrupts. 'Keith, I'd rather not talk about it.' She says it in a way that sounds less angry or cold, more like she's made a difficult decision during the night. She drinks some coffee. 'I'm going out in a minute. I've got a riding lesson this morning.' I'd forgotten it was Tuesday, her regular session. She'd told me, one day, she'd always wanted a horse ever since she was a little girl, so I ended up buying one for her birthday.

'Will you be home tonight?' she asks, picking up her sunglasses and keys.

'Yes, of course.'

'Okay, see you later. Dinner will be ready at seven.'

'Take care,' I call out as she opens the door to the garage, 'don't fall off!' I immediately regret being flippant; she's probably not in the mood for my sense of humour.

NINETEEN

ALISON

'Fuck him!' I shout the words out of the open sunroof as I drive to the stables. Why did I let myself get so angry last night? Why did I make my denial of his suggestion about Marcus and me sound so aggressive? And why did I blurt out my accusation of him and that high-class tart, Sylvia? (Of course I knew her name; I was just winding him up to see how he might react.) Now I'm the one feeling guilty – he practically guessed straight away what happened in Suzette with Marcus. I should have dismissed it as a laughable idea and pushed him further about his affair with his secretary. What a cliché! How tacky, although I can see how he would have been receptive to her obvious charms. One thing I've learnt about Keith, he has a straightforward outlook on life; he's never been what you might call one of life's sophisticated souls.

So many thoughts had raced through my head during the night. Should I contact Marcus and tell him about Keith's accusation? Tell him to deny it in case he bumped into Keith in town? I was pretty sure Marcus wouldn't initiate such a conversation. I admit a large part of me had wanted to see him again, but I'd resisted the temptation, telling myself that what happened in Suzette was strictly a "one-off", out-of-character and unexpected behaviour.

Well, bollocks to that. I really was angry with Keith, and getting into Marcus's bed was my revenge, although it helped enormously that I had always found him very attractive. And I could tell the feeling was mutual.

Once the panic of my denial to Keith had worn off, I'd begun to reflect on our marriage. I started to calculate in my head how long we'd been married – it came to twenty-eight years. The realisation dawned on me that I'd been married for four years longer than the age I was when I walked up the aisle on the arm of my proud father, my mother beaming with joy in the front row as her daughter was joined in holy matrimony to the man she'd always described as a "jolly good catch". And what had I got to show for my twenty-eight years of loyal wifedom? Two lovely children, of course, two human beings that I'd brought into the world and loved and cared for until they were able to stand on their own two feet – albeit with a certain amount of financial help from their father.

A lovely home? Yes, without doubt, although it was usually Keith who had decided when we should move and where we should live. And to be absolutely fair to him, he had always been a very generous provider. As the success of his business had multiplied, so had his desire to demonstrate how much he was worth. Even from the beginning, when he'd bought me the most expensive gifts he could afford, he had always wanted to impress. I wondered now if that desire was more to do with making an impression on the outside world than on his own family. I knew he'd be upset if he thought that was what I believed; he'd always prided himself on the motivation of "family first".

And what about the state of our relationship? Where had we arrived after twenty-eight years? I guessed the word "comfortable" came to mind. But isn't that how any couple of our vintage might describe themselves? Was there anything wrong with "comfortable"? Nothing at all, perhaps, but now I was beginning to wonder if I was actually happy. That thought stays with me as I arrive at the stables, but it soon fades as I busy myself getting my horse, Monty, ready for my lesson. I begin with a few gentle circuits of the dressage arena before my instructor, Valerie – 'Call me Val' – arrives; a butch-looking professional horsewoman who has a no-nonsense approach to tuition. She stands in the middle of the arena shouting out instructions as I manoeuvre Monty over the low jumps that make up the course. 'Come on, Alison,' she bellows, 'you're riding like a novice today.' I push Monty a bit harder and manage to jump three more barriers before I clip a pole that clatters to the ground. 'Again!' shouts Valerie. Her tone is not exactly encouraging, but it's enough to make me concentrate, and I manage another circuit with only eight faults. The hour of my lesson is soon over. I canter over towards Val and tug on the rein to halt Monty. She looks up, squinting in the sun. 'Not bad at all, Alison, not bad at all. I think you might be ready for that competition at Bicester we talked about. What do you say?' Praise indeed! To be honest, although I admit I did mention to Keith that I'd always wanted to own a horse, this whole horse-riding pursuit has taken me completely out of my comfort zone. I never dreamt I would be attempting to learn dressage; my initial thought was more about looking after a horse with the occasional gentle promenade in the countryside, all rather idyllic. But here I am, almost blushing at Val's praise and finding it difficult to say no to her suggestion.

'Yes, that would be great if you think I'm ready.' Valerie's weathered face almost breaks into a smile.

'Well, I wouldn't have mentioned it if I didn't think so,' she says in her sweetest voice. 'See you next week.' The rather unsettling thought suddenly enters my head that she might fancy me.

By the time I've settled Monty into his stable and I'm back in the car driving home, I've arrived at a decision. I have to tell myself the episode with Marcus in France was a one-off, not to be repeated, even if I do find it stimulating just thinking about it. And as for Keith and his secretary? Well, I have to admit it hurts that he's been unfaithful, but it's not a big enough reason to destroy our marriage. I'm guessing she'll get tired of him before long and move on. I smile to myself at the thought that maybe I should be casting an eye over his choice of secretary in the future.

TWENTY

2006 – MARCUS

I'm watching an episode of *The Sopranos* when the doorbell rings. I look at my watch – it's nine o'clock in the evening – and wonder who might be calling at this hour. I make my way to the hall and peer at the small screen mounted next to the entry phone. Recently, I'd installed a camera over the front door, not that I'm concerned about security as such, but we get bugged by people trying to sell stuff, or asking us to do surveys, or collecting donations for a charity, so I wanted to be able to see who was there without asking. That way, I could pretend to be out. I see the outline of a woman; slim, young-looking, holding what looks like a small bag, but there's not enough light from the street to make out any detail. Perhaps it's someone from the recording studio, although it seems late for that, and anyway they would have phoned first. Intrigued, I push the intercom button. 'Hullo?' I say, hoping the word and question is enough to elicit enough information for me to make a decision.

'May I speak with Marcus Kingsley, please?' Very polite, with a trace of an accent in her voice, but I can't place it.

'This is Marcus Kingsley,' I say, thinking this is all sounding rather formal. 'Do I know you?'

'Not exactly,' she replies, 'but I would like to meet you.' Her voice has more the tone of a statement than a request, but that might be the accent. I hesitate for a moment or two then decide it can't do any harm to let her in. 'Okay. I'll open the door for you. I'm on the top floor.' I open my door and wait for her to climb the stairs.

When she arrives, I can see she's older than I first thought, maybe late thirties, but the slim figure and jeans worn with a leather jacket give her a younger appearance. Even my sixty two-year-old eyes can appreciate she is very attractive. I step to one side and indicate with my arm to invite her inside. 'Please, come in. How can I help you? Are you from the studio?'

She looks at me, slightly puzzled by my question, and for the first time seems to lose her initial confidence. 'No, not a studio,' she replies. She looks into the apartment, hesitating before stepping over the threshold. 'It is, perhaps, a long story.'

'Well, you'd better come and sit down and tell me your story. Can I get you something to drink? A glass of wine? Some tea or coffee? Something stronger?'

'Yes,' she says, 'a tea would be very nice, thank you.' Again, that accent, which I'm beginning to think sounds more Germanic than anything else. While I busy myself in the kitchen making some tea and pouring myself a glass of wine, I sense her standing up and looking at the contents of my sitting room. She sits down again when I return with her tea.

'Perhaps you could tell me your name and how you found me.' I sit down on my sofa while she occupies the only armchair in my apartment.

'Those are two very good questions,' she replies, smiling. I begin to wonder if she's being enigmatic on purpose or whether it's just the correctness of her speech.

'Okay, why don't you start with your name?'

'My name is Margo, Margo Huber.'

'Ah, so you *are* German, right?'

'No, not correct,' she says, putting down her cup. 'I was born in St. Gallen, in the German-speaking part of Switzerland, but now I live in Zurich.'

'And what do you do in Zurich, Margo?' I'm not sure why I asked the question; just being polite, I suppose, while what I really want to know is why she'd been standing outside ringing my doorbell.

'I teach English in a school,' she replies, 'to children from twelve to sixteen,' as if I needed the extra information. At least it explains the excellent English. I sense her looking at me, not casually, but quite intently, as if she's searching for something. She takes another sip of tea. 'Does the name Huber mean anything to you?'

I stroke my chin while I try and recall anyone with that name. 'Sorry, I don't think so, should it?' She doesn't answer so I try my second question.

'So, you haven't told me how you found me.' She doesn't reply straight away. Instead, she asks if she may smoke a cigarette. It must be ten years since I stopped smoking, but I know I still have an ashtray in the kitchen. I'm not usually that keen on people smoking in the flat, the zeal of the ex-smoker, but I get the impression she's more nervous than she looks and could really use one. So, I fetch the ashtray and wait while she opens a silver pack of Marlboro and lights up.

'I have been in Spain, to Cunit. I met your friend Steven and his wife, Gloria. They gave me your address.'

Blimey! I think, *that's a coincidence, fancy meeting them*. Then I wonder why they didn't tell me about this young woman. I still don't understand why she wanted my address. Maybe she's a musician as well as a teacher, looking for some contacts in London. 'How are they? I haven't seen them for ages. They should have told me you were coming to London.'

She takes a long drag on her cigarette then taps the ash into the ashtray. 'I asked them not to tell you,' she says. That figures, I think, if she's looking for contacts, she'd rather use the direct approach than risk a rejection.

'I am not surprised you do not know the name Huber. It is a very common name in Switzerland. Perhaps the name Ingrid might, as you say, ring a bell?'

Again, I feel stumped. 'I'm sorry, no, I don't think so.'

'Perhaps these may help.' She delves into her bag, pulls out a wallet and hands me several photos. 'Ingrid Huber was in Cunit, in 1966, at the same time as you and your band?' She looks at me expectantly.

I look through the photos slowly. I see an attractive middle-aged woman, then the same woman with a young child, then a photo of Margo, obviously, with the woman in what looks like a hospital. The last photo is of a teenage girl, on a beach, wearing a bikini. I look more closely at the photo and suddenly I recognise her: the girl at the bar who smoked my cigarette, who took me for a swim at her parents' villa and afterwards had sex with me by the pool. I didn't want to admit I couldn't remember her name. 'Of course, Ingrid. Yes, now I do remember her. How do you know her? How is she? My God, it was such a long time ago.'

Margo stubs out her cigarette. 'Ingrid is dead. She was my mother.' She says it very calmly, as if she's been waiting to share this information for a long time.

'Jesus, I'm so sorry. Please excuse me, I didn't realise.' I can't think of anything else to say, although I'm still wondering why she felt the need to come all this way to tell me.

As if she's reading my mind, Margo looks directly at me. 'Before she died, my mother told me that you are my father.' The look on her face tells me she's deadly serious.

Suddenly the penny drops – her visit to Spain, the meeting with Steve and Gloria, the knock on the door, the afternoon by the pool with Ingrid. Shit, I have no idea what to say. 'I think I'm going to need one of your cigarettes,' is all I can manage.

Over another glass of wine for me and a whisky and water for her, Margo unfolds the story of how she has come to be sitting here in my flat. She tells me that about four weeks after her mother returned from Cunit, she realised she was pregnant – she was just seventeen. Eventually, she had to tell her parents, who were extremely angry and insisted on knowing the name of the father. But Ingrid refused to tell them. In truth, she didn't have much to go on, and so she was sent away to a distant relative in St. Gallen to have the baby, a daughter she called Margo. (It was at this point I couldn't help smiling about the similarity of our names. I also began to look at her more closely, searching for any similar features; maybe an echo of my younger self.) Ingrid's education had been interrupted by the pregnancy and birth of the child, but she had a talent for hairdressing, and as soon as she was able to support herself she moved to Zurich and raised Margo there, finding work and, after several years, opening her own salon. All the time she insisted that Margo study hard at school and pass the exams she would need to get into the university.

I listen to Margo talking, and fetch her another drink, storing up questions in my mind, but not asking. I can sense she needs to get her story out in one go.

After university, Margo travelled around Europe and the Far East, even getting as far as Australia, but after two years she returned to Zurich and found a position as a teacher, the post she still occupied today. She said this with a smile, explaining that she'd had enough of travelling, and besides, she was very fond of the children.

Eventually, I have to interrupt. 'But how did you find out I was your father? How long have you known?'

Margo lights another cigarette. Between us, we must have smoked half the pack. 'You can imagine as a child and as a teenager how often I asked my mother who my father was. But she refused to tell me. Maybe she was a bit embarrassed about the circumstances. Maybe she realised she didn't have much information to tell me. She would say, "One day I'll tell you, one day. It's not important; look at you, a beautiful young woman with a good education, the world at your feet." Of course, I would get angry with her. It's only natural for a child to want to know who both her parents are. But gradually the need subsided. I pushed the question to the back of my mind. I began to get on with my life, and I guess I started to believe maybe she was right after all.'

'So, what happened? What changed so much that she told you?'

She picks up her drink and takes a good swallow of my best malt. 'About six years ago, my mother was diagnosed with cancer, a cancer of the breast. She had good treatment, the best she could afford, and it seemed as if the treatment had been successful. But the cancer returned last year. This time, it was everywhere.'

I let her take her time. She pulls a tissue from her bag and wipes away a tear. 'Two days before she died, she was in a hospice by this time. She pulled me towards her bed. "Margo," she said, "do you still want to know about your father?" She began to tell me all about meeting you in Spain, how you played in a band, how she persuaded you to go for a swim at the villa... how my life began in a moment of teenage passion.' Margo pauses for a moment before speaking again, her tears now dry. 'Then I began my detective work.' She's smiling now. 'I waited until my next summer vacation and decided to go to Spain, to visit Cunit. I thought maybe I could find the bar, or perhaps someone in the village might remember an English band playing there.'

I couldn't help smiling. 'Well, that was a bit of a long shot, if you don't mind me saying so. It must have been nearly forty years ago.'

'Yes.' She was smiling now too. 'I felt rather stupid walking around the village asking if anyone remembered these events. But eventually I found someone who recalled a bar owned by some English people, where they used to play music. He took me to the place where the bar used to be and explained that the building was now a bakery and coffee shop. He could see I was disappointed, but then he said he knew there was a couple living in the village, an English man and his wife, a famous singer. I could see he was thinking perhaps music was the connection I was looking for. And so, that's how I found Steven and Gloria. Of course, I'd heard of her. She is very popular at home, but I had no idea she was living in Spain. The man showed me the house where they live, and I knocked on the door. I asked the woman who answered if there was anyone who could help me with information about the bar. She asked me to wait and then a man, Steven, as it turned out, came to the door. Like you, he was a bit unsure to start with, probably thinking I was a fan of his wife and wondering how I'd found out where they lived. But I explained why I was in Cunit, about my mother dying, and why I needed some information about you. He was very kind and asked me to come in and then, the next thing, he's introducing me to his wife, the famous Gloria. It was quite surreal to see her in the flesh. I mean, I've seen her on TV and in videos, but here she was, shaking my hand and asking me if I would like something to drink. We sat in their beautiful courtyard and I told them the whole story, just like I've told you, but insisting that if they knew where you live, they shouldn't let you know about me. They were both very kind to me, and I can tell by your reaction to my news, they kept their word. Steven told me a few things about you. He joked that you were always the good-looking one in the band, that you had something of a reputation with "the ladies", as he described it. But he also said you'd been a good friend, how you'd helped get Gloria's career started. I got the impression he was rather sad you hadn't kept in touch with each other.'

Margo seems to relax as she finishes speaking, while I've got a thousand questions running around in my head. I glance at my watch; it's getting on for midnight. 'Look, it's really late. You've given me an awful lot to think about. How long are you in London? Can we talk about this again tomorrow? Where are you staying? I'll phone for a cab.'

She stands up, tall, and stretches her arms. I can see she gets her height from me. 'Yes, of course, tomorrow. I would like that.' She gives me the address of the hostel where she is staying and I realise it's only a few streets away.

'Come on, I'll walk you, it'll be quicker than waiting for a taxi.' We stroll around the square, side by side, not really talking, and take a short cut towards Ladbroke Grove. I'd never noticed the hostel before. It looks like the kind of place you'd expect to find full of overseas students; a rundown apartment block, a bit dingy. At the main entrance, I suggest I call round for her in the morning, about ten-thirty, 'If that's okay with you.'

'Yes, of course, that would be perfect,' she replies, smiling. I'm not sure whether to shake her hand, kiss her, or give her a hug. We settle on a slightly awkward hug. She turns towards the doorway and I watch as she disappears inside.

Walking back to the flat, I begin to assemble the events of the evening. This Swiss girl comes to see me, tells me all about Spain and her mother who died, then drops the bombshell that I'm her father. I mean, it all sounds very plausible and I have a clear memory of the sex by the pool, but is that enough to make me her father? Jesus! It was the sixties, everyone was shagging everyone. Wasn't every girl on the pill in those days? What proof has she got that I'm her father? As much as her story intrigues me, and as much as I might feel strangely excited to find out I have a child, I'm going to have to find a way of explaining that we need to prove it, maybe take a blood test or something.

So, here I am, the next morning, standing outside the hostel, sheltering under my umbrella. I've rung the bell and been told to wait by the manager. It's the kind of place that discourages the "students" from having visitors, probably to prevent them having "non-paying" guests. After a few minutes, Margo pulls open the door and gives me a warm smile. She looks much the same as last night; jeans, a pale blue shirt and the leather jacket across her shoulders. In the daylight, with her cropped hair and fresh face, she looks younger, almost boyish. She steps under the umbrella. 'Good morning,' she says, 'is this your typical London rain?'

'Only in the summer.' I laugh. 'It's supposed to be good for the complexion. Coffee?' She smiles and nods an eager approval. She slips her arm inside mine, a simple gesture that makes me feel as if she has already accepted me. We head off towards Bayswater Road to find the nearest Costa, and settle down with two flat whites on the only remaining sofa.

'Look, Margo,' I begin, as she stirs sugar into her coffee, 'before we go any further, I need to ask you something.'

She raises her eyes and stops stirring. 'What is it?'

I shift my position on the sofa, leaning in towards her. 'Last night, your story, everything you told me. It all sounds perfectly reasonable, but I just wonder...'

'You mean, how do you know I'm your daughter?' The directness of her reply makes me sit back. 'I, too, have thought of this. I can see how strange this situation must be for you. I think it is only natural for a man to ask this question.' She takes a sip of her drink, puts down the cup and replies, softly. 'My mother told me, also, she had only been with one boy before, a boy from her school, a few months before she saw you. But she admitted it was her idea to invite you to the villa. She knew she wanted you.' Her gaze drifts towards the window; she waits for me to speak. I feel an impulse to lean across and take her hand. She turns to face me, a tear forming in the corner of her eye. I continue to speak.

'Look, this is big for both of us. I can see how important it is for you, but it is for me, too. Let me ask you a question, what would you do if you were in my position?'

She smiles and wipes away the tear. 'I would probably want some proof.' Now we are both smiling.

'Exactly,' I say, 'and that's exactly what we're going to do. I'll find out what needs to be done, maybe some kind of DNA test, and then we'll know for sure. Would you agree to that?'

She strokes the back of my hand. 'Of course I do.' Getting this delicate issue out into the open has the effect of making us both feel more at ease. It seems as if we have jumped an important hurdle and I decide to move the conversation along.

'So, you didn't say how long you are going to be in London.'

She puts down her cup and dabs her mouth on a paper napkin. 'Well, even though I knew your address, I didn't know if I would find you at home, or how it would be… our meeting. I have only two more nights at the hostel then I must return to Zurich. I have to get ready for the new term at school.'

'So soon?' A mild panic runs through me. I've only just met her, this young woman who I've suddenly found out might be my daughter, and now she's leaving in two days' time. 'Listen, why don't you come and stay with me? I can easily turn my office back into a bedroom. It wouldn't be a problem at all.'

Margo looks at me sympathetically. 'You are very kind but no, I don't think so. It's too soon. I have a lot to think about. You must have too.' She's right, of course. She's being a lot more sensible than me. She notices the look of concern on my face. 'There's a half-term in a few weeks time, perhaps I could come and see you? It will give you time to find out whatever test we need to take.' It dawns on me she's had a lot more time to think about having a father than I have about a daughter.

'Yes, that would make a lot of sense. I'll get something organised and then I can let you know.' I relax back into the sofa, feeling as if we're becoming more comfortable with each other. 'So, you've told me where you live and what your job is and how you found me. How about your own life? Do you have a boyfriend? Or are you married? You didn't say.'

Margo begins to stand up. She doesn't reply to my question but asks instead, 'Shall we have another coffee?'

While she orders at the counter, I look out of the window and watch the world go by. A world where yesterday I didn't have a daughter and now, it seems, I do. It's stopped raining and I can see my face reflected in the window. I'm smiling – which, thinking about it, must look strangely odd to anyone walking by.

Margo puts the two fresh cups on the low table and sits down. 'I did have a boyfriend for a long time. Actually, we lived together for nearly two years, then something rather different happened.'

I resist the temptation to say *What?* and wait for her to continue.

She looks directly at me. 'I realised I prefer girls to boys.'

Jesus! I think, *what a waste*, then immediately regret the thought; the kind of sexist, chauvinist comment you'd expect from an old-fashioned male; nothing like me at all, well, maybe a bit. Of course, it's beginning to make sense now; the fresh face, the cropped hairstyle, the leather jacket and jeans – she still looks very pretty, very attractive, but I can see how she might appeal to another woman. She's waiting for me to respond to her admission. 'So,' I say, trying to look as blasé as possible, 'if that's the case, I'll rephrase my question. Have you got a girlfriend?'

Now she's laughing. 'Somehow, Marcus, I knew you'd say that!' She begins to tell me how she met a Frenchwoman, Naomi, on a singles holiday, how they became attracted to each other. 'And now we live together in my apartment in Zurich, with our dog, Rocket,' she adds.

I'm trying to think of something funny to say about the dog's name, but I ask instead, 'And what does Naomi think about you looking for your father?'

For a moment, Margo looks pensive. 'Well, she supports me, of course, but I think, also, she's worried I might lose my feelings for her if I did find my father.'

'And will you?' I ask.

'No, of course not. I love her very much.' We both remain silent for a while, lost in our own thoughts.

'Come on,' I say, standing up, 'the sun's out, let's go for a walk in the park, then I'm going to take you for a nice, long, expensive lunch. I think we've got a lot of catching-up to do.'

TWENTY-ONE

MARGO

(TRANSLATED FROM THE ORIGINAL SWISS-GERMAN)

The Eurostar emerges from the tunnel and we are soon speeding through the French countryside. Fields and farms flash by; we race past cars and trucks on the motorway that runs parallel to the track. I listen to the muffled sound of the wheels, feel the train sway around a long curve, my head leaning against the window as I think about my journey to London to find Marcus.

I'm amazed at how well he took the news. Maybe because he's single and doesn't have to explain to a wife or girlfriend that he suddenly has a daughter. It seemed to me, once he'd got over the initial shock, that he rather liked the idea. I knew at some point, even with the information I'd given him about my mother, he would want some kind of proof, so it was just as well I preempted that question by suggesting we take a medical test. He seemed quite willing to do that.

All the while we were talking, I was trying to find some similarity between us. Even at his age – sixtyish? – I would have to admit he is still an attractive man. I can see why his friend in Spain said he had a reputation with *the ladies*. But it was not only a physical feature I was searching for, but also, perhaps, a gesture or an expression that I might recognise as one of my own. Didn't someone say that those things were more to do with nature, not nurture? It was obvious to me we have the same nose and the same cleft chin. And we share the same broad hands; no fine, piano-playing fingers for either of us! What did surprise me was the way he moved his hands when he spoke, emphasising words with gestures, more like an Italian. It's something I do too. How did that happen?

I have to smile when I recall the look on his face when I told him I was gay. I could tell he was surprised and maybe a little disappointed; he was probably thinking of me as a straight woman, but he recovered well enough to make a joke about me having a girlfriend. All in all, I left with the impression Marcus is a very kind man, very *sympa* as the French would say, someone I feel comfortable with, someone I would be happy to have as a father. Thinking of having a father does feel strange to me after all those years of wondering and then not really caring. But now that I've met him, my own flesh and blood, I'm beginning to understand the connection that can exist between a daughter and her father.

The drinks trolley approaches and I order a gin and tonic. I feel a desire to celebrate my new status as a daughter. I raise my glass to my reflection in the window and make a silent toast to my mother, to say thank you for finally telling me about my father.

I settle back into my seat, close my eyes and think about Naomi. I hope she's going to be at the station to meet me;

I wonder how she's going to take my news. I didn't say too much when I called her mobile. When we get home, I'm going to sit her down with a bottle of our favourite wine and tell her it's not going to make any difference to my feelings for her. I think she might have been hoping that if I did find my father, I might be disappointed; that it would be an anti-climax; that I'd forget all about him. Most of all, I want her to understand that, even though I may have found my father, it won't change how strongly I feel about her. Actually, I have a good feeling she and Marcus would get on really well.

I finish my drink, lean back and close my eyes. I come to the conclusion it would be a good idea if Naomi and I both go back to London at half-term.

I wonder if Marcus can fit a double bed into his spare room.

TWENTY-TWO

2007 – ALISON

'Whaaat?' I'm trying to hear what Marcus has just said on the phone, but the twins are making a helluva row in the pool. Sophie dropped them off yesterday and now I'm on lifeguard duty while they play in the shallow end, squirting each other with water pistols. 'I'm sorry, Marcus, it's a bit noisy here. Can you say that again?' I concentrate on what Marcus is saying, still keeping one eye on the children. 'You've got a daughter? Oh my God, how did that happen? Sorry, I didn't mean that. I mean, how did you find out?' I didn't want to add, *How the hell do you know she's yours?* But the thought crossed my mind. I listen while he tells me how this young woman turns up on his doorstep and says she's his daughter. How she explains all about her mother, about the episode in Cunit, how she was certain Marcus was the father, how she managed to track him down in London. And how they've had the results of a DNA test to prove she really is his daughter.

'Oh my God, Marcus,' this time more gently, 'how do you feel about it?' As the words come out of his mouth, the smile in his voice is enough to tell me he's rather happy about the situation. 'Look, Marcus, I've got my hands rather full at the moment with Sophie's twins, but I'd really like to talk to you. I'm coming up to London on Tuesday. Perhaps we could meet for lunch. You can tell me all about your mystery daughter. I want all the details.' Marcus laughs and says he'd love to meet for lunch – it's been long overdue – and suggests a place to eat, saying he'll text me the address. I end the call and tap the phone against my chin, mulling over what he's just told me. Golly, Marcus a father, who'd have thought it?

Mister commitment-phobe with a child. Well, grown woman to be precise. *Lucky girl*, I think to myself. She couldn't have found a nicer man to have as a father.

'Come on, my darlings!' I shout at the twins. 'It's time to get out before you drown each other.' They giggle and turn in unison towards me, unleashing a volley of water from their pistols in my direction, soaking my dress in seconds. *You little buggers*, I think, but don't say. Mina, our housekeeper, steps onto the terrace carrying a tray with tea for me and lemon squash for the kids. I'm sure they'd rather have a can of Coke but Sophie doesn't like them having "fizzy" drinks. I think she'd prefer it if they drank green tea, like her. Mina helps me get the kids dry and takes them indoors to get dressed.

As I sip my tea and think about what Marcus has just told me, the old feelings for him begin to rise in my mind; thinking about the time I seduced him in Suzette, regretting that I didn't make more of an effort to see him after Keith's affair with his secretary. But, here I am. I didn't leave Keith. I'm living in this beautiful mansion, with its acres of fields and woods, and its lake, and the tennis court and heated pool. Of course, I soon realised Keith wasn't capable of having just the one affair. The confident young man who courted me, the "good catch" who had my mother practically wetting her knickers, has turned into the kind of wealthy entrepreneur, like those Russian oligarchs, from whom an attractive gold-digging woman is never far away. They don't even have to work for him anymore; there are always plenty of likely candidates at the fashionable charity events he likes to attend, eyeing him up, working out how much he's worth, how much they can get out of him. Of course, he'd never stoop to paying cash for sex, but there will always be a nice piece of jewellery, or a seat on a private jet, maybe a discreet weekend away, to pay them off before the novelty wears thin.

I gaze at the ripples in the pool and wonder, not for the first time, why I put up with it. God knows it would be simple to get a divorce, it would be easy to get proof of his infidelities, and I would be entitled to a large chunk of his wealth. But where would that leave me? Rattling around in this place on my own, the children probably hating me for divorcing their darling daddy, the one who spoilt them when they were young and continues to spoil them in their adult lives. It's not as if I've been entirely innocent myself. I don't mean sleeping with Marcus, that was a while ago, but there was that young man at the stables, the visiting professional rider, who offered to give me a private lesson; the one who delighted in pulling off my jodphurs as we rolled, literally, in the hay. Or the guy that Keith sent to the house to demonstrate the Mercedes he wanted me to have; where we stopped in a country park and he lent across me to show me the controls and our lips met. Thinking about it, I'm sure it was just the way he smelt that suddenly turned me on. Suffice to say, I didn't buy the car; that would have been too much of an impulse purchase.

But these were isolated moments, certainly not affairs, just times when I felt neglected by Keith and, if I'm honest, feeling that what was sauce for the goose was also good for the gander. Does that make me an unfaithful wife? On balance, I think I'm better off staying where I am. Keith and I have an unwritten understanding about his behaviour; between what he does away from home and how we live together, respecting one another. I've seen him through some tough times with his business ventures. He's been a good father to Jake and Sophie. He can be incredibly generous, too generous sometimes, in my opinion. We still have our intimate moments, albeit not so often; I guess we still love each other. He understands I know him better than anyone else. I can't help smiling to myself that if we lived in Paris this would seem like a very normal arrangement for any long-married couple.

The afternoon sun has nearly dried my dress. I stand up and walk away from the pool, leaving the wet towels and tea things for Mina to tidy up later. I open the gate and enter the walled garden that I persuaded Keith to let me design. I wanted it to be a mixture of traditional English country-house borders combined with more formal beds of cutting flowers and herbs. I'm rather pleased with the result. I stroll along a path of white gravel, trailing my fingers through the lavender border, savouring the smell that reminds me of Provence. At this time of year, the garden is full of the blues and whites I love the most. I pass under an archway of iceberg roses, pausing to smell their delicate perfume. I wave to Ben, our gardener, who is on a mission to deadhead every flower and pull out any weeds that dare to enter "his" domain. He waves back and lifts up a basket of cut blooms to show me he has carried out the task I left for him this morning. I climb the steps from the garden onto the flagstone terrace that runs the length of the house. The folding double doors are open, allowing the summer breeze to circulate through the interior. I step into the large sitting room, taking in the comfortable furniture, the huge stone fireplace, the walls covered in an eclectic mix of artwork, framed photos on every flat surface. I can't help thinking it looks like something you'd see in an interior design magazine, no surprise really since Keith hired the best designer he could find. We call it the Family Room, although it seems ages since we actually sat in here as a family; maybe Christmas, two years ago?

I climb the stairs to my study on the second floor. The window looks out over "my" garden to the wooded parkland and lake that persuaded Keith to purchase the property. I think he felt it gave him a certain status, in the manner of those Victorian industrialists who invested in large estates to mimic the landed gentry. Unlike the rest of the house, the room is a jumble of personal belongings. Books are piled on top of the piano, paintings rest against the walls, waiting to be hung. Photos of the children, and their children, are propped up on bookshelves and windowsills. Items of comfortable clothing and sheets of music compete for space on the chairs. A chaise longue nestles against one wall, covered in a tartan blanket, somewhere I can fall asleep on a winter's afternoon. I see my reflection in the art-deco cheval mirror. I turn sideways, straighten my back, pull in my tummy. My hair, with a little help from Lucy at Silvio's, is still chestnut brown; my legs, thanks to all that exercise swimming and riding, are still in good shape – mmm, altogether not too bad for an "old girl".

My antique desk, with its inlaid leather surface, is pushed up against the window. I notice that someone, Keith presumably, has left a pile of invitations on the desk for me to sign. They're the invitations to my 60th birthday party – the party I'd rather not have but that Keith insists we give. I glance through the accompanying sheets of paper, put together by his PA, listing the names of all the invitees. Most of them I don't recognise, probably clients and senior staff of Keith's. A few I recognise as friends we've made on holidays, or old neighbours, parents of friends of the children, a smattering of fellow students from my university days, the friendships I've kept up with Christmas and birthday cards. Then I notice the name Marcus Kingsley halfway down the second sheet. I sheaf through the pile until I find his invitation. I notice Keith has already signed them, so I guess this is his way of telling me to get a move on. I pull open a drawer, take out my favourite fountain pen, then add my signature to Marcus's invitation, putting "xx" after my name, and a handwritten note suggesting it might be an excuse to get the band together again. I slide the invitation into its envelope, seal it, close my eyes and kiss it. The thought of meeting Marcus for lunch is beginning to feel rather exciting.

TWENTY-THREE

STEVE

When I opened the invitation to Alison's 60th, I had to ask myself if I really wanted to go. I mean, I know she's my sister and all that, but the memory of what happened twenty years ago is still fresh in my mind. And the covering note suggesting we get the band back together again was enough for me to wish that Gloria might, "unfortunately", be away on tour. But, as I said, she is my sister, so I talked it over with Gloria and she said of course we must go. She's much more family-oriented than me, something to do with being Brazilian, I guess. We thought about taking the children but decided against it. Since the whole "Gloria" phenomenon took off, I'd begun to take more of a back seat on the touring front. I found I was enjoying the travelling and performing less and less, preferring to be more involved with arranging the music. Besides, it was never hard to find good guitarists willing to join a world-class act. It meant I could spend more time at home with the kids when they were young. This year, they've both started new schools in Barcelona; they love taking the hi-speed train into the city, and Consuela, our housekeeper, is here to ensure not only that they catch the train in the morning, but that they do their homework at night. So, it was an easy decision to leave them at home.

I cast my mind back to the last time Alison came to visit. It must be at least three years ago. She and Keith had combined a business trip to Madrid with viewing some properties on the coast. God knows why they, or more accurately *he*, wanted to buy a villa in Spain when they had such a beautiful house in Provence. Knowing Keith, there was probably some kind of tax deal going on. Anyway, the houses they wanted to see were not far away, so Alison asked if they could come and stay here while their estate agent drove them around. Since we'd first arrived in Cunit all those years ago, and Gloria had become more successful, we'd moved house a couple of times but always stayed in the town. Now we live in what were once three townhouses which we had knocked into one, so there was always plenty of space. From time to time, we'd thought of moving out of the village, maybe moving into a bigger place in the hills, but we liked the place. It was handy for the beach, and the locals, by and large, left us alone. I think they were rather proud to have an international star living amongst them and felt protective of Gloria's privacy.

Between you and me, I'd always thought Keith was a bit of a prick, even from the early days of Alexander's Relations. Granted, when we started out, he was good at getting us gigs, but he always fancied himself as a bit of a rock star on stage and, if I'm being honest, he was a rubbish guitarist. Of course, his business has become hugely successful. He's probably a multi-millionaire, but boy, does he let you know it! In some ways, I'm amazed

Alison has put up with him for all these years; maybe he has qualities that are hidden from the rest of the world. For me, the last straw was her fortieth birthday, the one where I fell off the stage, which, to this day, I swear was not my fault. If it hadn't been for the fact that she was my sister, I'm convinced he would have thrown me out of the house for spoiling his big moment in front of his mates. He probably would have enjoyed that, too. As you can probably tell, I'm not his biggest fan.

So, here we are, twenty years down the track, with another invitation to a party for Alison, courtesy of Keith. The fact that he wants us to play again is bad enough, but I'm already picturing the scene where he will make a big fuss of "inviting" Gloria onto the stage, just so he can show off again. She, bless her, will take it in her stride and, with the fixed smile I've seen before, agree to perform with "Keith's" band.

I'm reminding her of this as we unpack in the guest suite that Alison insisted we occupy, even though Keith, I'm sure, would have preferred to give it to one of his important clients. I can imagine the dilemma he must have faced between giving up the suite to his "loser" brother-in-law or allowing Gloria, the international star, to have it. In the end, his need for status and universal approval would have won.

'If he's going to ask you to sing then at least we'd better have a rehearsal.' The idea of, let's face it, an amateur band providing the backing for Gloria is beginning to worry me.

'Don't worry, Steven,' – she's always called me Steven, never Steve – 'I've already spoken to Alison and she and I are going to put together an arrangement, then, when the others arrive, we'll have a proper rehearsal.' She smiles and strokes my cheek. 'Don't worry, we can still make it look spontaneous, just for Keith. I know you two don't get along but this whole event is important for him, too.' Believe me, this woman has a genuine heart of pure gold.

Looking out of the window, I see a car emerging from the wooded copse, throwing up dust along the long driveway that curves up to the house. It stops in front of the columns flanking the wide stone steps that lead to the main entrance. I watch as the occupants of the car get out and one of Keith's flunkeys fusses around with their luggage.

'Gloria, look, there's Marco and Dave. And that must be Margo and her girlfriend.' She comes over to the window, squeezing in front of me, leaning forward to get a better view.

'Oh, isn't that wonderful! I'm so happy for Marcus.' Ever since Margo came to see us and told us her story about looking for Marcus, we've been following the progress of the paternity via news from Alison. We'd heard the tests had come back positive and that Marcus had accepted, with genuine delight, that he now has a daughter. "Absolutely chuffed" was how Alison described it.

'Come on, my darling,' Gloria is tugging my arm, 'let's go down and see them. You know how hard it was keeping Margo's visit a secret from Marcus. I want to tell them both how thrilled I am that her story turned out to be true. And I want to give Dave a big hug, too!' Gloria is in her element; it's what she does best, spreading joy.

By the time we get downstairs, Marco and the others have already joined Alison in the vast kitchen. She is supervising tea for everyone while distributing plates of homemade cakes. Everyone is smiling, chatting away, looking relaxed, except Naomi, who seems quite overwhelmed by the occasion and is clutching Margo's hand. As soon as Margo spots us, she rushes over and practically jumps into Gloria's arms. 'I'm so happy to see you, you too, Steven.' She kisses both of us, warmly. Now she's laughing, 'Come, please, I want you to meet my father,' as if we didn't know the whole story. She pulls us towards Marco and the four of us are soon engulfed in a group hug. 'And this is my girlfriend, Naomi, but I guess you know that already.' We both give her a kiss on the cheek and tell her it's lovely to meet her at last. She smiles and begins to look more relaxed.

Now it's Dave's turn for the big greeting. The cake in his hand is halfway to his mouth as Gloria moves to hug him. 'Dave, it's wonderful to see you again.'

He drops the cake on the table and returns the embrace, smiling at me over Gloria's shoulder. 'Good to see you too, Gloria, and you, mate.' Dave and I shake hands. It's been a while since I saw him; he looks thinner. 'Brought your kit with you?'

'Of course, never without it,' he replies.

Everyone is chatting and busy catching up when Keith pokes his head around the door. For a brief moment, the chatter stops as heads turn towards him. I can see he feels awkward, as if he's intruded on a private conversation; not really one of the gang. But he recovers quickly, bustling into the kitchen. 'Hey! Here you are, starting without me. Any of that cake left for me, love?' He moves around the kitchen, greeting everyone with bear-like hugs. He looks like he's put on some weight since I last saw him; his ruddy cheeks give the impression of someone with high blood pressure rather than an outdoor life. He munches on a large chunk of cake. 'So, here we all are. It's great you could be here to help me celebrate Alison's, whisper it softly, sixtieth birthday! Doesn't she look great?' He squeezes her waist and gives her a crumbly kiss on the cheek. She looks at the floor, slightly embarrassed. She's never liked being the centre of attention. Keith turns towards Gloria. 'Gloria, darling, it's wonderful you are here. We are truly honoured you've agreed to perform with our humble band. My guests are going to get such a wonderful surprise when I announce you're here to sing for us.' Not exactly true, I think to myself, more like so you can show off in front of your mates.

She smiles and nods towards him. 'It will be my pleasure, Keith.'

He beams back and claps his hands. 'Okay, everyone, Alison tells me we're going to have a rehearsal later. I've got a few more things to organise,' he pretends to hide his face from Alison, tapping his nose with his finger, 'so, shall we say six o'clock, before dinner?' With that, he hurries out of the kitchen, leaving us to continue our conversations. I glance over towards Alison. She raises her eyebrows with a resigned look, as if to say, *He doesn't change, does he?*

Dave, bless him, has spent the afternoon setting up our gear on stage in the giant marquee that has been erected next to the pool. Gloria's decided to have a rest, so I've been wandering round the estate. Although it's not my "thing", I have to admit the house and its grounds are looking stunning, like something out of an estate agent's brochure. You have to hand it to Keith; he's made sure everything looks perfect for the party. There's not a blade of grass out of place.

'Hey, Dave, how's it going?' I ask as he tapes one of the cables firmly to the stage. 'Don't want anyone tripping over this time.'

He smiles back. 'I always knew you weren't pissed.'

We both laugh at the painful memory. 'So, how are you? I heard you had a bit of a health scare.'

'What? The prostate thing? No, that's all sorted now, never fitter.' He taps himself in the vague region of his waist. 'Just have a check-up every six months.' He fixes another strip of gaffer tape. 'And you, you okay?'

'Absolutely fine,' I reply, 'although I find it hard to give up the fags, one of the simple pleasures in life in my opinion, but I am cutting down.'

'Yeah, well,' says Dave, 'I guess we're all getting older and trying to be more sensible.'

'Amen to that,' I say. I give Dave a hand setting up the rest of the gear, tuning a couple of guitars and making sure the amps and speakers are in sync. We go about this task in silence, nodding and smiling to each other, with the occasional thumbs-up when we're satisfied.

I don't really know why I'm still feeling nervous about the gig tomorrow. Possibly it's because we haven't played together in such a long while. Maybe it's because I feel responsible for letting Gloria get talked into performing. 'Don't worry so much, Steven,' she's already told me, 'it will be fine. Don't you remember when we first met, and I was singing in those small clubs? It will be just like that, only this time I'm hoping more people will recognise me.' We both laugh at the memory of those early days, before Marco helped us get Gloria's career off the ground.

'See you later, Dave,' I say as I head out of the marquee.

'You too, mate,' he replies, continuing to fuss over his drum kit.

As arranged, the five of us, plus Gloria, gather together at 6pm for our rehearsal. Keith has already decided he wants the band to play some of our sixties covers before he invites Gloria onto the stage; to build up the "surprise factor", as he calls it. No one has any objections. Ali runs through the arrangement she and Gloria have worked out. This would usually be my department, but I'd been happy to let get them on with it. I'm sure Ali was pleased to rekindle some of her musical prowess, and it gave them both the chance to have a good old natter. It's easy for me to pick up my part, and Dave soon gets into the rhythm. It's a number I've played a hundred times before, but I'm still impressed how Alison has included a couple of simple changes to the arrangement, something I file away for future reference. Poor Keith is struggling to keep up. It's obvious he's okay to play our old numbers, but give him something new to learn and it's clear he's out of his depth. He keeps stopping and asking Ali to explain the chords again, which she does, patiently, while the rest of us try to ignore him. Gloria, as only she can, comes to the rescue. 'Keith, darling,' she smiles at him, 'don't worry about a few chords. No one will really notice. Besides, you have an important job to make the announcements, then I would like you to sing the chorus with me. I think that would be fun, don't you?' The look of anger and frustration on Keith's face is quickly replaced by a beaming smile of contentment, in the dawning knowledge that he will be duetting in front of all his business pals with an international star. I can see the weight lift from his shoulders, although he can't resist saying, with false modesty, 'Well, if you insist.' The rest of us can't help laughing and, give him his due, even Keith can see the funny side of it. We continue with the rehearsal, everyone now in a better mood.

By the time we've run through a few more numbers, Marco and the others feel happy we've done enough to put on a performance. To be honest, I'm surprised it's gone so well. Then Marco admits he's been practising at home and Alison and Dave own up, too. I get the feeling they didn't want to let me, or more likely, Gloria, down. We have a laugh, although Keith doesn't find it so amusing. Maybe he didn't get the practising message from Ali. Perhaps now is not the best time to tell him what's been on my mind, but I decide to go ahead anyway. 'Hey, Keith, I know you've made Ali's party a black tie affair, but there's no way I'm standing up here dressed like a bloody penguin.'

He gives me a frosty stare, the kind he probably reserves for an employee who might dare to question one of his decisions. 'Jesus, Steve, why do you always have to be so bloody difficult? Can't you just...'

But Ali interrupts before he can finish. 'I think he's right, Keith. It'll be fun to change clothes; otherwise, we'll look like a bunch of guests who've ambled onto the stage. It'll make us look more "professional".' She winks at me behind Keith's back.

I can sense the cogs in Keith's brain weighing up the options, then a smile breaks out across his face. 'You're absolutely right, my darling You can all wear whatever you like. I don't mind, it'll be fun. But I shall stick with black tie. After all, I am the host.'

Typical Keith; always has to have the last word.

We gather later for supper in their farmhouse-style kitchen, seated around the huge oak table. With her big party coming up the next day, Ali has decided this dinner should be just for family and close friends. Sophie and Jake have arrived with partners and children. A couple of Ali's friends from college are already here. Marco is chatting to Sophie; Margo and Naomi, who seem inseparable, have their heads together in close conversation; Dave is helping, politely, to pass food around. Gloria sits next to Keith; I think her declared mission is to keep him happy and boost his confidence. She has a knack for reading people and putting them at ease. She's already told me she believes, despite his bluster, Keith can still feel insecure. Maybe that's what driven him to be so successful. Anyway, he's looking more relaxed than I've seen him since we arrived, enjoying the company of Gloria, opening another bottle of wine. I have to give the old bugger some credit; he does have a spectacular wine cellar. I glance across the table and catch Ali's eye. I raise my glass to salute her and she returns the gesture; we both smile, brother to sister. I can't help thinking this would be the kind of birthday celebration she would have preferred: an informal evening with the people she loves.

I don't need to open the curtains to know the sun is already shining. I check my mobile to see if there is any message from Spain, but the screen is blank. I guess that means Consuela has got everything under control at home. I think about sending the kids a message but decide against it. They'll be on their way to school and, besides, we'll talk to them later before the party gets under way. I get out of bed and pad towards the window, opening the curtain slowly. Sure enough, it looks like it's going to be another fabulous day. Who said there's no such thing as an English summer? Everything looks perfect; not surprising since Ali and Keith have had an army of people working inside and outside ever since we've been here. Even so, I can see Keith is already up and about, talking to one of the gardeners. I smile at the thought that someone will get a bollocking if so much as a weed is visible.

'Honey, what time is it?' Gloria turns over and buries her face in the pillow. She's not a morning person, probably the result of years of touring and performing.

'It's not time to get up yet, sweetheart,' I reply. 'Go back to sleep. I'm going to have a wander around then I'll bring you some breakfast.' She makes a sigh of pleasure to indicate this is a good idea; no further conversation required.

'Good morning, birthday girl,' I say as I enter the kitchen and see Ali drinking coffee. 'Ready for your big day?'

She smiles and pours a mug for me. 'As ready as I'll ever be. Between you and me, I'll be glad when it's all over.' I walk over and give her a hug. Funny, we never used to be a "huggy" family; I guess our parents weren't very demonstrative towards us children, but I've noticed, since I've got older, I'm much more likely to be affectionate. Must be Gloria's influence.

'Don't worry,' I say, stroking her shoulder, 'you'll be fine once it gets started. Keith's got everything under control and you only have to be the centre of attention for one day, then you can go back to being the shy young sister I used to know.'

She gives me a nudge in the ribs. 'You can talk, Mister moody guy, you could go for weeks without saying anything!' We laugh and clink our mugs in mutual appreciation of each over. 'What do you fancy for breakfast?' she asks, turning towards the catering-size stove.

'The full English, of course,' I reply. 'What else?'

The glass doors from the terrace slide open and the two lovers, Margo and Naomi, draped in towels, step into the kitchen. 'Morning, ladies,' says Ali, 'how's the pool?'

Margo grins back. 'Fabulous, so refreshing.' She looks over at me. 'Are you going in too, Steven?'

'Maybe later,' I laugh, 'when it gets a bit warmer. Don't forget you guys live in Switzerland and I live in Spain. It has to be a lot hotter than this before I get in the water. Why don't you go and wake your father and ask him if he wants a swim? Tell him he's had enough beauty sleep.' We've been teasing both of them since we found out, emphasising the words "father" and "daughter", much to their, and our, amusement.

I don't think I've actually heard Margo say "Dad", but I guess it's a lot easier to say "Marcus" when you don't find out who your father is until you're in your thirties. Mind you, I've seen the look of pride on Marco's face when he introduces Margo as his daughter; I couldn't be happier for him.

I wander out into the garden. That's an understatement; it's more like an estate of lawns, flowerbeds, orchard, pool, tennis court, ornamental trees and a lake big enough to have a boathouse. I amble along paths that meander through the grounds, pausing to smell a flower or touch a leaf. I make my way around the edge of the lake and find a bench in the sunshine. I look back at the house; there's no other way to describe it, it's fucking enormous; a beautiful, symmetrical Georgian pile. How much it might be worth wouldn't impress me, but I have to admire the sheer elegance of the place. I hear a shout of 'Hi, Steve,' and turn to see Keith approaching from the other end of the lake. I give him a wave and wait until he arrives and sits down, heavily, onto the bench. As I said before, he and I have never been mates, but still, I can always be polite. 'Wow, Keith, this is some place you have. I've never seen it from here before, it looks beautiful. You must be really proud. Worth all the hard work, eh?'

He nods and smiles. 'Thanks, Steve, I appreciate you saying that. It's taken a lot of effort and cost a lot of dough, but I think it's been worth it. I feel as if I'm making a contribution to the landscape.' He pauses, like he's trying to find the right phrase, then his face lights up, 'As if I've made my mark.'

We sit there for a while admiring the scenery then Keith nudges my arm and points towards the middle of the lake. 'See that pontoon? That's for tonight's firework display, but don't say a word to Ali. It's a big secret, her birthday finale.' He's laughing and clapping his hands like a delighted schoolboy.

'Don't worry,' I say, 'I won't tell a soul.'

'Good man,' he says, standing up and patting me on the back. 'Must get on, see you later!'

I sit there for a while; I shut my eyes and let the sun warm my face. I think about lighting a cigarette but decide it's too early. Besides, I'm supposed to be giving up. I hear another voice. 'Hey, Steve, are you asleep?' I open my eyes and see Marco.

'So, you're up at last,' I say, 'not swimming?'

He laughs and sits down. 'Not bloody likely, far too early for me. I told those girls I'd go in later, maybe.' Marco waves his arm in the general direction of the house and grounds. 'What do you make of all this, Steve?'

I pause before replying. 'Well, you can't help being impressed, can you, although it's not exactly my cup of tea. I guess it says everything you think of about Keith. It's big, it's on a grand scale, it says wealth, it says status but, and here I have to give him due credit, it does have a lot of style. He's just been telling me how he feels he's put his mark on the landscape, and I can't argue with that.'

Marco gazes out over the lake. 'And what about Ali, what does she think about it all? Do you think she's happy here?'

I smile. 'I don't suppose she really thinks much about it. She would probably say it's just another one of Keith's "projects". I don't imagine she really minds where they live. She's not a material girl.' I look at Marco's face. 'Why? Do you think she's unhappy?' I'm puzzled as to why he would ask the question.

He doesn't answer for a while then says, 'I dunno, she and Keith have been together a long time, but sometimes I wonder if they're on the same wavelength.'

'Well,' I say, 'I'm no expert on relationships. Maybe they've reached a point where they're just comfortable with each other. Besides, we don't see that much of them.

You probably know them better than I do. Has Ali said anything to you?'

Marco doesn't offer a reply, which makes me wonder if he knows more than he's telling me. 'Anyway,' I say, going back to the original question, 'I'm sure she loves the garden she's created and the fact there's enough room in the house for the kids and all the grandkids.'

Marco laughs. 'Enough room? Jesus, I bet there must be rooms in the house she's never even seen yet!' Marco always manages to make me smile; he has a gift for putting people at ease, for finding something amusing to say. I sometimes think he would have made a good diplomat.

'And what about you?' I say. 'How's it going with having a daughter who has a girlfriend?'

Marco stretches and puts his arm along the back of the wooden bench. 'I tell you what, Steve, finding out about Margo has been one of the best things in my life. I mean, you know me, I've never really been the marrying type, but to find out I have a daughter, after all these years, well, it's been amazing.' He pauses a while. 'Don't get me wrong, it was a bit of a shock to start with, you know, someone coming along and upsetting my selfish bachelor world, but I can honestly say I couldn't be happier. I must admit the "girlfriend" thing came as a surprise but, you know what? It doesn't change anything at all. I can see they adore each other.' Marco turns towards me and smiles. 'And here's some breaking news, Steve, they've decided they want to have a baby. To be quite honest, I don't quite know how they intend to go about that, but it's top secret, so keep it under your hat.'

I can't help smiling to myself; it's the second time this morning I've been asked to keep a secret. Why does everyone want to confide in me? Do I have such a trusting face? Don't they know I'm bound to tell Gloria? We have no secrets between us. 'So, does this mean you'll be Grandad Marco?'

'Fuck off,' he says, 'I'm far too young to be a "grandad". They'll have to think of something else to call me.'

We sit on the bench watching the activity on the other side of the lake, the final preparations for Ali's party. There's a small army of people carrying trays of glasses, erecting tables, arranging flowers, laying cables, fixing lights, setting up what looks like a mobile kitchen. 'I tell you what, Marco, you have to hand it to Keith. He certainly knows how to organise a party.'

He smiles. 'You've got that right, Steve. Remember how he used to organise us in the band? We'd probably still be playing in your dad's garage if he hadn't got us some gigs.' We both laugh, knowing, reluctantly, it might be true.

'What are you doing for the rest of the morning?' asks Marco.

'Nothing much,' I reply. 'Why?'

'Fancy having a go at clay pigeon shooting? Keith said he was going to set it up. Come on, it might be fun. We can pretend we're the local squires out for a morning's shoot.'

The idea of shooting anything is not really my scene, but I haven't got a better idea. 'Yeah, sure. Why not? Let's give it a go.'

TWENTY-FOUR

ALISON

Marcus is already seated at the table when I enter the restaurant. It wasn't a place I knew at all. Somewhere in the city that used to be a bank but had been transformed into a Parisienne-style brasserie. I thank the waitress as she leads me to the table and smile as Marcus stands to greet me. We exchange kisses on both cheeks, French-style, as if to suit our surroundings.

'Hullo, Marcus,' I say, 'it's so good to see you, it's been ages.'

'And you too,' he replies. 'You're looking gorgeous, as always.'

'Oh, stop it, you big smoothie! I bet you say that to all your girlfriends.' We sit down and as I unfold the linen napkin, I feel flattered that he noticed how I look. Little does he know how many times I changed my clothes this morning before I could decide on the "right" look. God! I'm beginning to feel like I'm on my first date.

'Shall we have a drink while we decide what to eat? How about a kir royale?'

'Mmm, that sounds perfect,' I reply. 'After all, you do have something to celebrate.' Marcus orders the drinks and we spend a while looking at the menu. To be completely honest, I'm not really taking much notice of any of the choices, but it all looks delicious.

'So, Marcus,' I begin, 'it was all rather hectic when we spoke on the phone. Tell me again how you found out you were a father. You mentioned something about a girl turning up on your doorstep and some story about her mother in Cunit. What was that all about?'

Marcus gives me a rueful smile and begins to tell me the whole story over again. Our drinks arrive while he's telling me, and we pause to smile and raise our glasses before he continues. When he gets to the part about Margo living with her lover, another girl, I can't help thinking how very twenty-first century it all sounds. Typical of Marcus to be right on-trend. Our waitress is hovering, ready for our order. 'So, what do you fancy?' says Marcus. 'I can recommend the steak or the lobster.'

I wave my hand at the menu. 'Oh, I can't decide, it all looks delicious. Why don't you order for me?' Marcus laughs and tells the waitress I'll have what he's having. While he studies the wine list, I look across the table to see if his new parental status has changed him at all. I decide he still looks the same youthful Marcus, with maybe a few grey streaks showing in his amazingly good head of hair. Unlike Keith, who is already going bald.

'You haven't really told me how you *feel* about becoming a father, or even, dare I say, a *parent*.'

Marcus gives me a look of mock horror. 'Well, I don't know about the parenting side, bit late for me to start telling her to do her homework, or not to stay out too late. But as for being a father? To tell the truth, it took a while for the idea to sink in, but now, I must admit, I'm enjoying my new role. You know me well enough, Ali, to know I haven't exactly been the marrying kind, so the idea of having children, or even wanting them, never really occurred to me.'

'Don't tell me after all the girls you've slept with there aren't one or two Marcus sprogs around.'

'Jesus,' he says, that look of horror again. 'Don't even go there!' The waiter brings the wine and pours a glass for both of us as Marcus waves away his tasting option.

'Here's to parenthood, at whatever stage of life,' I say, raising my glass to him.

Marcus returns the gesture. 'And here's to you and yours. From what I've seen of them, you've managed to raise two lovely children, not to mention grandchildren, Grandma.'

I aim a mock kick at him under the table. 'Don't you dare use that word,' I whisper. 'I'm far too young to be one of those.'

We both laugh. 'Well, you certainly don't look like one,' says Marcus, 'but I bet you adore them, all the same.'

Our meal arrives, a lobster salad to start with followed by fillet steak. Marcus has ordered a large plate of French fries which we share. I concentrate on eating for a while. I'm not used to drinking at lunchtime and feel the sensible thing is to absorb some of the alcohol. Marcus continues to entertain me with more stories about Margo, about his trip to visit her in Zurich, about meeting the girlfriend. Then he drops the bombshell: 'And now they're talking about having a baby!'

For a moment, my fork is frozen between plate and mouth. I don't know what to say, trying to gauge from his expression whether he thinks this a good idea or not. I get the impression he's not at all concerned about the situation. I gather my thoughts. 'So,' I say, 'does that mean we'll have to start calling you Grandad?'

Marcus laughs and raises his glass. *'Touché.'*

We share a pudding, profiteroles, something I would never choose myself, so I allow Marcus to devour most of them. 'How do you manage to stay so slim?' I ask, as he licks the last speck of chocolate from his spoon.

'I'll let you into a secret,' he says, leaning back and patting his stomach, 'I've joined a gym, go three times a week. I've been working on my "core", at least that's what my instructor calls it.'

I can't stop myself from laughing. 'I'm trying to imagine you in your Lycra gym wear. Isn't it all a bit… revealing?'

'God forbid!' says Marcus. 'No, nothing like that at all. Just a t-shirt and a pair of shorts, although they have to be black, of course, just to fit in with the rest of the gym bunnies.'

'Well, it's obviously doing you a lot of good. You're looking very fit, in both senses of the word, if I may say so.' I realise for the first time that I sound like I'm flirting. It must be the wine.

'Why don't we move over to the bar and have a coffee?' suggests Marcus. 'It'll be quieter there.'

'Good idea,' I say, standing up from the table. 'Can you order an espresso for me, please, while I nip to the loo.'

By the time I've finished freshening up and checking out how I look, I find Marcus relaxing on a small sofa. There are two coffees on the low table in front of him and what look suspiciously like two glasses of cognac. I squeeze in beside him on the sofa, suddenly aware of my thigh pressing against his. 'Well, this is cosy, isn't it? I hope you're not trying to get me drunk,' I say, trying to make light of the situation, despite knowing a time when I'd pressed my body up against his, willingly, without the help of alcohol.

Marcus turns his head and gives me one of his hundred-watt smiles. 'Not my style,' he says, offering me one of the cognacs while raising his own glass. 'What shall we drink to?'

For the first time since I arrived, I look into his eyes, properly, to see if I can fathom what he is thinking. I sense that he may be remembering our time in Suzette, too. 'How about, to us?' I say, softly. I take a sip of the golden liquid, feeling its warmth as it descends, spreading a kind of glow. I feel the words forming in my head, words I've wanted to say for a long time. 'Marcus, can I ask you something?'

He looks back at me, his warm smile slowly changing to a look of concern. 'Of course, Ali, what is it?'

I open my mouth to speak but nothing emerges for a moment or two. 'Why didn't you ever get in touch with me again after, you know, Suzette?'

His look of concern changes to a bashful grin. 'Jesus, Ali, don't think it didn't cross my mind, many times.' He reaches over and takes my hand. 'But after Keith returned to the villa, it felt like you'd decided it was a "one-off", something you regretted. I know you denied it at the time, but I still couldn't shake the idea that it was revenge for your suspicions about Keith. And, at the end of the day, you were still married to him and he is supposed to be a mate of mine, even if he can be a bit of a boring old fart at times. I mean, what would you have wanted? To carry on an affair behind his back?'

I stroke his hand, realising that everything he has said is true, but sad too. 'I'm sorry, Marcus,' I begin, 'I shouldn't have asked, it was unfair of me...'

Before I can continue, he squeezes my hand then puts his arm around me. 'No need to apologise,' he says. 'I'm glad you asked.' He smiles. 'It's funny, in a way.'

'What's funny?' I say.

Marcus sips his cognac then looks at me. 'Remember when the band went to Cunit? Believe it or not, I had serious designs on you that summer. My simple plan was to get you into bed. But you always looked so serious, surrounded by all those admiring French boys, and I certainly didn't get any indication you were interested in me at all. And then I met Ingrid. Who knows what might have happened if I'd managed to get you to sleep with me?'

I smile back at him. 'Thanks, that's very sweet of you to let me know, after all this time, that I was the object of your desire. My loss, I guess, but then, we wouldn't be sitting here talking about your lovely daughter, would we?'

I sip my cognac and wonder what reaction I was expecting from Marcus in answer to my question. That he'd admit he'd agonised about contacting me after Suzette? That he'd thought about me constantly? (Or at least as often as I'd thought about him.) That he would suggest we grab a taxi and head back to his place to make love again? I realise I'm beginning to think like a schoolgirl with a crush. I sigh and look at my watch. 'Marcus, I guess I ought to be going. It's been really lovely seeing you again. And thank you for such a delicious lunch.'

Is that a look of disappointment or sadness in his eyes? Would the "old" Marcus have been suggesting we head back to his place, too? Instead, he gives my hand a squeeze. 'It's been great to see you too, Ali, it's been far too long. You must let me know when you're coming up to town again, maybe next time Margo is over. I'd love you to meet her.'

Marcus settles the bill, waving away my offer to go halves. 'Certainly not,' he says, smiling. 'My treat, but if it'll make you feel better, you can take me to lunch next time.' I file away that thought for another day while we head for the door. Marcus hails a cab and offers to drop me off at Waterloo. I gaze out of the window, looking at the shopfronts, watching people rushing about their business, another world, I think, from my quiet life in the country. It makes me think I should try and get up to town more often. Perhaps another opportunity to see him? 'Anyway,' he says, interrupting my daydream, 'how is the old entrepreneur, still building his empire?'

I smile, thinking about the contrast between these two men in my life. Keith, my husband: hunter, gatherer, wealthy provider, overweight and balding; and Marcus: cool, handsome, relaxed, the eternal bachelor. 'Yes, still the same old Keith, still working all hours, always on the go. You know what he's like.'

'Well, I hope he's not neglecting you,' says Marcus, softly. It's the first time all day that he's even given a hint of flirting with me. I look at him to see if there is a suggestion in his voice. Something that might indicate he's thinking we could, perhaps, end up in bed this afternoon. But he's just smiling, with a look that says that moment has passed. The cab pulls up to a halt in front of the station and I slide across the seat to reach the door. Then, changing my mind, I edge back to Marcus and kiss him on the lips. 'Thanks again, Marcus, I've had a really lovely time.'

'Me too,' he replies.

As I walk to catch my train, I turn to wave goodbye, but the taxi has already merged into the London traffic and disappeared.

TWENTY-FIVE

MARCUS

By the time Steve and I, under the careful tuition of Keith's estate manager (who knew he even had one?) have blasted enough clay pigeons to satisfy our egos, we decide it must be time for lunch. When we arrive back at the house, we find everyone either lounging around the pool or helping themselves to an enormous buffet. Alison had told us earlier lunch would be a 'simple, *al fresco* affair by the pool, weather permitting,' but this looks to me more like the kind of buffet one would expect to find at a five-star hotel. I help myself to a plate of king prawns, pour a glass of the palest pink rosé and find a comfortable wicker armchair next to Margo. 'Hi, Papa,' she says, smiling up at me from her sunbed. She's decided she can't bring herself to say "Daddy" but she thinks "Marcus" sounds too familiar, so, for the time being, I'm "Papa". Actually, I rather like it; sounds a lot more sophisticated than "Dad", especially with her accent. She and Naomi are lying close to each other, wearing what I can only describe as tiny bikinis. As a man who has enjoyed many a sunny day on a beach admiring attractive women, I'm finding it difficult to separate the image of the stunning young woman beside me from the reality that she is my grown-up daughter. As if she's reading my thoughts, Margo smiles again, teasing. 'Papa, I hope you're not checking us out.' She turns over and indicates to Naomi to apply more lotion to her back.

'Sorry, darling, no, of course not,' I say, hoping to hell my sunglasses hide my embarrassment. 'I was just wondering which bits of me you have inherited.'

Margo turns her head towards me. 'You mean, you don't think I look like my mother? Surely you haven't forgotten her!' The mock indignation in her voice tells me she's still teasing.

'Well, it *was* over thirty years ago and yes, she *was* beautiful, that I do remember.' With eyes closed, her smile tells me she's satisfied with my answer.

She lifts herself onto her elbows. 'So, you want to know what I've inherited from you? Well, that's easy,' she says, 'you gave me these,' pointing at her nose and chin, 'and these,' she waves her hands. 'When I came to your apartment, I looked at you and knew for sure you were my father.'

I bend awkwardly and kneel beside her, kissing her lightly on the head. 'Bless you, my child.' We both giggle; even Naomi joins in. 'So, what are you doing after lunch? More swimming?'

'We are going riding with Alison. We thought it was a good idea to take her mind off all these preparations, so she is going to take us to her riding school. She has arranged for us to have a horse each, two "gentle" horses, she said.'

'Are you sure that's a good idea?' I say, sounding like the concerned father. 'We don't want anyone breaking any bones. Have you been riding before?'

'No, not really,' says Margo, 'but Naomi is keen and said she'll look after me. And Alison is an expert horsewoman, so I'm sure it will be fine.'

I glance over at Naomi, looking for some reassurance. She's a sweet soul who doesn't usually say very much but she smiles at me. 'Don't worry, Mr Kingsley. I will take good care of Margo.' I've tried to explain to her that she doesn't have to call me "Mr Kingsley", to call me "Marcus" instead, but her polite Swiss reserve and the still recent knowledge that Margo found the father she was looking for, has made her somewhat reticent in my company. I can understand she feels there's now a third person in their relationship, that I might come between her and Margo, but I've tried to reassure her that as far as I'm concerned, I have accepted that she and Margo are a couple and couldn't be happier for them.

'Well, that's good to know, Naomi. I'm sure you will.'

I decide to spend the rest of the afternoon reading. I've just started Jonathan Franzen's *The Corrections* and am finding its story of a dysfunctional American family highly entertaining and beautifully written. I wonder idly why the name "John" so often appears on my list of favourite authors – Steinbeck, Irvine and Wain, the underrated English author of *Hurry on Down* and *Strike the Father Dead*, whose anti-establishment books impressed and influenced me in my late teens and early twenties.

I have no problem with losing myself in a good book for hours; of all the pastimes one can find to do on a holiday, I think reading is one of the best. Besides, I've a feeling it's going to be a long night, especially with the band performing later, so I need very little excuse to retire to my room. Despite my reputation for being a "social animal", I'm perfectly happy to spend time in my own company.

The sound of Margo and Naomi laughing in the room next to mine wakes me from what has clearly been an unexpected afternoon nap, the book still open on my chest. I'm not usually one for sleeping in the daytime, imagining that's what "old" people do. I tell myself it must have been the wine at lunchtime rather than admit it might have something to do with my age, too. Without putting my shoes on, I pad along the corridor to their room and knock on the door. 'Can I come in?' Their laughter stops, as if they've been caught in the middle of doing something.

'Who is it?' one of them asks. I don't recognise the voice; they both sound very similar with their Swiss accents.

'It's me.' I hesitate. 'Marcus.'

'Come in, Papa, the door isn't locked.' They both look hot and sweaty, in need of a shower.

'How was the riding? Nobody fall off?'

'We had a great time,' says Margo, smiling. She puts her arm around Naomi and rests her head on her girlfriend's shoulder. 'Alison and Naomi made sure I stayed in the saddle, so no accidents to report.' It's the first time I've seen them being anything approaching intimate. They look so loving with each other, so natural and pleased to share their happiness in front of me. 'What time do we need to be ready?' asks Margo, peeling off her t-shirt. 'We both need a shower and plenty of time to get dressed.'

I turn away and pretend to study a painting on the wall. I recognise it as one of David Farrant's much sought-after café scenes. 'Dinner's at eight with drinks first, so you've got plenty of time. I'll call for you around seven, okay?'

'See,' says Margo, giving Naomi a kiss on her nose, 'plenty of time.' They both giggle and hug each other. I wonder if that's why they were laughing when I'd knocked on their door.

The invitation had requested black tie. To my mind, the idea of getting dressed up like a penguin, on a warm summer's evening, in the twenty-first century, seemed a bit unnecessary, a tad too formal, but Keith had insisted. And as Keith was paying for this major "do", I guess he had the right to decide what everyone should wear. Besides, it would only be temporary attire as far as Ali, Steve, Dave and myself were concerned. We'd already agreed we were not going to perform dressed up to the nines. Despite our persuasions, Keith, obstinately, had said he was not going to change out of his dinner suit when he went on stage. He said he was going to remain dressed formally, as host for the evening. I've a feeling I wasn't alone in thinking he also wanted to remind everyone that he was "in charge". Good old Keith, always the Boss.

After a shower and a shave, I pull out my DJ from the suit carrier hanging in the wardrobe. Checking the pockets of the jacket to see if I can find my bow tie, I extract a folded card. It's the invitation to a dinner I attended two years ago, so the last time I'd worn a dinner suit. Luckily, I find the tie in another pocket and finish getting dressed, fiddling awkwardly with shirt studs and cufflinks. I run my fingers through my hair and check my appearance in the long mirror. *Not bad*, I decide, and if I half close my eyes, I look, maybe, ten years younger. *Yeah, who are you kidding, boyo?* wagging a finger at my reflection.

I check my watch; it's just gone seven, so I decide it's time to call for the girls. When she opens the door, Margo thrusts a glass of champagne into my hand. 'Celebrating already, are we?' I say, wondering not only where they'd got the bottle but also how they'd managed to keep it ice cold.

As if reading my mind, Margo explains, 'Alison sent it up for us, thought we might be thirsty after our ride.' Judging by their smiling faces and the half-empty bottle in the ice bucket, I get the impression the party has already started. They both look amazing. Naomi is wearing a pale blue sleeveless dress, with a high neckline. It looks like silk and finishes halfway down her bare, tanned thighs. Not quite "black tie", I think, but she looks stunning. Margo, bless her, has made the effort to keep to the formal invitation. She's sporting a black dinner suit, also in silk, with slim-fitting jacket and trousers, a soft white shirt and a thin black tie, hanging loose from the collar.

I smile and step towards them, holding my arms out to give them a hug. 'You look gorgeous, both of you. I'm really happy for you, I mean it.' We share a slightly awkward hug, holding our champagne glasses out to one side. 'Come on,' I say. 'Drink up, it's time to join the party.'

It looks like most of the guests have already arrived, milling about in the early evening sunshine on the lawns and the terrace in front of the pool. I notice the safety cover has been put in place, probably to avoid anyone falling, or jumping, in later. A posse of waiters circulates amongst the groups of guests, refilling champagne flutes and offering canapés from silver trays. I spot Steve and Gloria standing to one side, Gloria with her back to the crowd, a trick she's learnt in the past to avoid being recognised. I steer the girls towards them; they look relieved to see us, Gloria quickly starting a conversation with Margo and Naomi. I get the impression she's enjoying the part she played in getting me and Margo together.

'It's got to be said, mate, you scrub up very well.' I tease Steve, knowing how he must be cringing having to dress up in a formal suit.

'Don't make me laugh,' he says. 'I had to hire this, you know. It reminds me of all those twenty-first birthday parties we used to play at. It's like stepping back in time.'

Steve offers me a cigarette, which I decline, and lights one himself. Looking around, I can't see anyone else smoking; another sign of the times.

I see Alison making her way through the throng towards us. 'Hi, birthday girl,' I say, giving her a kiss on the cheek. 'Look at us, don't we all look lovely? You look fabulous!'

Unusually for Ali, her hair is piled up in a chic style; she's wearing a classic, deep purple floor-length evening dress with what looks like several thousand pounds worth of diamonds glittering around her neck and on her ears. She smiles and squeezes my arm. 'Thank you, kind sir.' She looks around, slightly nervous. 'I can't believe all these people. I don't know half of them. Typical of Keith to invite the world and his wife.'

'Obviously, you don't know how popular you are,' I reply. 'Here, have some fizz and relax.' I grab a glass from a passing waiter and thrust it into her hand. 'Happy birthday, Ali.'

The others join in and we all clink glasses. 'Thanks, Marcus. I needed that,' says Ali, draining her glass. 'I guess I'd better go and circulate. I'll see you all later.' She swirls away and disappears into the crowd.

By this time, Dave has joined us, and he's not alone.

'Hullo, everyone,' he says, giving us a funny little wave. 'Er, this is Samantha. She's an old friend of Ali's, from uni. We've been chatting this afternoon. Seems like we're both here on our own so I invited her to join us, if that's okay.'

Samantha looks slightly embarrassed by the introduction but smiles and gives us a similar wave. 'Of course, mate, no problem at all,' I say, offering a hand to Dave's date. 'Lovely to meet you, do come and join us.' While the others continue the introductions, I give Dave a wink and a thumbs-up. 'Ali's not sitting with us,' I explain, 'so there's a spare place at our table.' Previously, Ali had expressed a preference for sitting with the rest of the band, but Keith had demanded she sit with him on the "top" table. Fair enough, really, he *is* throwing this party for *her*, after all. He'd also asked Gloria to sit next to him, but she'd put her foot down and said, politely, she would prefer to sit with her husband. She really didn't want to be Keith's trophy celebrity guest.

We carry on talking and drinking until an announcement comes over the PA. 'Ladies and gentlemen, would you please make your way into the marquee where dinner will be served.' We join the crowd of guests beginning to move slowly towards the marquee, some of them causing a bottleneck as they peer at the table plan placed at the entrance. Inside the marquee, having found their correct table, people perform the "dance", amongst much muttering and laughter, of moving around the table to find their place name. Eventually, everyone is in the right place, Keith says a short, simple grace, and we all sit down. The walls and ceiling of the marquee have been decorated with strands of white fairy lights, a beautiful arrangement of flowers is set on each table, late-evening sunlight continues to shine through the planed glass-effect windows, and an attractive young harpist is on stage playing soft background music. The effect is quite magical. Soon, waiters are filling glasses, everyone relaxes, and a buzz of chatter fills the tent. You have to hand it to Keith; he certainly knows how to put on a good show.

As the food begins to arrive, the noise level drops; everyone keen to soak up some of their pre-dinner drinks. The meal itself is "safe" but delicious function fare. Smoked salmon, sour cream and blinis with a spoonful of caviar, for starters, followed by roast lamb and an Eton Mess for dessert, with port and cheese for those still hungry. The service is smooth yet unhurried, the wine continues to flow – Keith, again, has spared no expense – and the overall mood is one of satisfied contentment. As the plates are cleared and coffee is served, Keith stands with a microphone in his hand and taps a spoon against a glass. The harpist rests her instrument and the chatter, slowly, dies down.

'Good evening, everyone,' he begins. 'It's a real pleasure to see so many people here this evening to help me celebrate the birthday of my lovely wife, Ali. It would be ungallant of me to tell you how old she is, but I guess you will have worked that out for yourselves from the invitation,' a ripple of laughter spreads through the marquee, 'but I think you will agree she doesn't look anything like her age and, as I keep being told, sixty *is* the new forty. Oops, sorry, love, let the cat out of the bag there,' he says, in mock horror. Again, more laughter, with Ali smiling awkwardly and looking somewhat embarrassed. Keith, holding up a hand to quieten his audience, continues. 'Don't worry, this is not going to be a long speech, but I couldn't let the occasion pass without saying how lucky I have been to have spent nearly forty of those years with this amazing woman, a woman who looks as beautiful now as she did on the day of our first date. To be absolutely honest, she didn't really want to go out with me,' he pauses, 'but her mother insisted.'

This time the room erupts in genuine laughter and Ali joins in, nodding her head as if to say, *You're absolutely right!*

Keith turns towards Ali, smiling. 'Darling, I know you don't like surprises, but I couldn't let the occasion go by without getting you a birthday cake, so I hope you'll like this one.' He waves an arm towards the marquee entrance and, right on cue, a piper, in full highland kit, appears playing *Happy Birthday*. He's followed by a waiter carrying a tray on which a large decorated cake is topped off with a huge sparkling firework. As the piper works his way through the tables, everyone begins to clap and sing *Happy Birthday*. By the time the cake arrives at the top table, Ali is looking genuinely happy and surprised. She stands to kiss Keith on the cheek and gives a wave of thanks to the room. Keith, looking very pleased with himself, again turns to the guests. 'Ladies and gentlemen, please charge your glasses and join me in wishing Alison a very happy birthday.' As requested, everyone stands and, with much waving of glasses, a collective 'Happy birthday' issues around the tented room. As we all sit down, Keith, still standing, continues to speak. 'And now, lovely guests, please feel free to circulate while we clear some of the tables to make room for the dancefloor. For those of you who haven't heard us before, I hope you're looking forward to hearing my old band, Alexander's Relations, play for you shortly. In the meantime, I suggest we get this party well and truly started.' He turns towards the stage behind him. 'Take it away, Mr DJ.' As he says this, a curtain across a corner of the stage drops down to reveal a young guy standing behind the twin turntables of a sound deck. The first loud beats bursting from the speakers seem to act as a signal for people to start drifting outside; whether to escape the sudden noise or just to enjoy some fresh air, it's hard to decide.

Dave, Steve and I make our excuses to go and get changed ready for the gig, leaving Gloria and the girls and Dave's new friend, who says she prefers to be called Sam, to continue chatting. I always find it amazing how four women who hardly know each other can still find a way to have an intense discussion about important topics of the day, when four men, in the same situation, would struggle to hold a conversation beyond sport, the weather or sex.

Thirty minutes later, I'm standing at the back of the marquee waiting for the others. As it's a warm evening, I've chosen to wear a pair of loose linen trousers topped with a bright Hawaiian shirt. I have to smile when Steve turns up, sporting black leather jeans and a faded t-shirt. 'Just like the old days, eh? You don't change, do you?'

He looks me up and down. 'And what are you supposed to be? You look like you're on a bloody cruise!' He delves into his pocket and pulls out what is obviously a joint.

'Blimey, where'd you get that?' I ask, partly surprised but mainly interested.

'Don't ask,' he says, 'want some?' Before I can reply, he's already sparked up and drawing heavily on it before passing it to me. I can't remember the last time I smoked any weed, must be at least twenty years ago, but I accept the joint, take a hit then cough, much to my embarrassment, as I exhale.

'Jesus,' I say, 'that's strong stuff.'

Steve smiles down at me from his six foot plus. 'Amateur,' he says.

Dave and Ali come jogging hand in hand around the corner of the marquee. 'Are we late? Took me ages to get changed, sorry.' she pants. Dave, true to drummers everywhere, is wearing running shoes, baggy shorts and a faded sleeveless vest with a picture of Fidel Castro smoking a cigar on the front, perhaps a reference to his sometime leftist leanings. Meanwhile, Ali has transformed herself back to her twenties. Her hair is long and loose, a fringe almost covers her eyes and she's wearing her "trademark" black polo neck sweater, short check skirt and black tights.

'Wow!' I exclaim, slowly, probably showing the effect of the joint I've been enjoying. 'You look fantastic, Ali. Absolutely, bloody fantastic.'

She looks back at me and teases, 'Well, I'll take that as a compliment, shall I?'

We're standing around in a huddle wondering what to do next, when Keith's face, looking rather flustered, appears through one of the rolled-up windows of the marquee. 'Come on, you lot, get yourselves in here, we're on!'

TWENTY-SIX

DAVE

Seeing Keith's ruddy face poke through the window of the marquee reminds me of the Punch and Judy tent I used to see on our holidays at the seaside. The nasty man with the stick always seemed to have an angry red face. I must have been five or six years old; it was certainly before my father finally left us. We used to take a caravan on a site near Lulworth Cove. I remember walking back from the farm shop on unsteady legs, proudly clutching a jug of fresh milk. There were campfires and sing-songs in the evenings, and I'd go bathing in the crystal-clear sea at Durdle Door. I remember a pair of knitted trunks that rubbed against my legs and absorbed so much water they almost fell down when I stood up. How come every day seemed to be so sunny on our summer holidays? I don't remember it ever raining at all, although thinking about it now, with a career spent studying weather, I'm pretty sure it must have rained at least once during an English fortnight in August.

The four of us hurry round the front of the marquee and make our way onto the stage. The DJ continues to play dance music while we get ourselves and our instruments organised. Looking out from behind my drum kit, I see a small crowd on the dancefloor, some moving enthusiastically, others just swaying in time to the music. No one seems that keen to hear us. Keith checks to see if we're all ready, then gives a nod to the guy on the turntables, his signal to make an announcement. The DJ fades the music and pulls the mike towards him. 'Ladies and gentlemen, that's all from me for the time being. If you've been taking a breather, please make your way back to the marquee, because it's the moment I know you've all been waiting for.' He grins at Keith and makes a beckoning gesture in the general direction of the marquee entrance. 'It's my enormous pleasure to introduce, on this special, one-off occasion, the return of that famous band from the sixties, Alexander's Relations!'

Jesus, I think, *we've never had an introduction like that before. Bit over the top if you ask me.* As the DJ finishes speaking, I tap my sticks four times and we head off into *Green Onions*. Given that we haven't had a lot of time to practise, it's amazing we all manage to start together. After the first couple of numbers, more people begin to enter the marquee, and the place is soon full. I can see groups of people just standing and watching in the background, probably curious to see this band of, shall we say, their contemporaries, playing the kind of music they grew up with. Before long, more people appear on the dancefloor. It's typical of any middle-class, middle-aged group of people; everyone needs the help of a few drinks to overcome their natural reserve. We continue to bash out more numbers, the audience begins to join in the songs, and everyone is genuinely amused when Marcus and Ali do their *I Got You, Babe* duet. As the last chords of a very noisy *Hi, Ho, Silver Lining* subside, Keith steps towards the centre of the stage and raises his hands. It takes a while for people to notice that he wants to say something. 'Are you having a good time?' he asks, beaming. The response is not great, so he asks again, louder. 'Are you having a good time?' This time, there's an enthusiastic cheer, mainly coming from a boisterous group at the front. 'Ladies and gentlemen,' he begins, 'it is my privilege to welcome to the stage someone you will recognise immediately. An international superstar who also just happens to be the wife of our wonderful lead guitarist, Steve.'

Blimey, Keith, I think to myself, *unlike you to give any credit to Steve, he's never been one of your best mates before now.* Keith continues. 'Please put your hands together and give a big, warm welcome to...' he pauses then shouts, 'Gloria!'

Heads begin to turn as she makes her way to the stage and everyone starts to clap. I can sense a mood of genuine excitement, touched with disbelief, as Gloria steps onto the stage and stands next to Keith. She puts her hands together in prayer-like fashion and bows towards the audience. She smiles at Keith, waves her arms to the rest of us and says into the mike, 'Shall we do this?' At the rehearsal, Steve, being Gloria's former musical director, had suggested that he should accompany her along with Ali and myself – basically the most accomplished musicians. Marcus wasn't too bothered by this, being our vocalist, but you can imagine how far Keith's nose was put out of joint. If anyone was going to be on stage with her, it was bloody well going to be him! Gloria, to her eternal credit, had calmed him down, suggesting he might like to join her in a duet because 'My English is not so good.' This seemed to pacify him so that now, while he's waiting for his moment in the spotlight, he stays on stage, guitar round his neck, pretending to be part of the backing.

Gloria's performance is having the effect of turning a noisy crowd of party guests into a respectful, engaged audience. There's silence while she sings and an appreciative round of applause as she finishes each song. Admittedly, there are a few chuckles as Keith steps up, with much encouragement from Gloria, for his duet but, give him his due, he manages to keep in time and stay in tune. She finishes her performance with an upbeat version of one of her international hits, encouraging the audience to carry on dancing, even managing to steer Keith around the stage with a few samba steps. He can't believe it, waving to his guests, beaming, with a look of pure pleasure on his flushed face.

After the excitement of Gloria's performance, the five of us continue playing our practised repertoire of hits from the sixties. People are dancing and drinking and singing along; it takes me back to our gigs at that time, same kind of audience, just older now, like the rest of us. I spot Marco's daughter and her girlfriend dancing energetically near the front of the stage, Margo looking impressed with this unexpected version of her father. Further away, I can see my new friend, Samantha, swaying to the music, looking happy, like she's in her own little bubble. Earlier in the day, she'd been telling me how she and Ali had got on really well at university, how she'd decided to switch her degree to study medicine, how she'd developed a career as a clinical psychiatrist, married another doctor, got divorced, and how much she regretted not having children. It felt like we had a lot in common and, for the first time in a long time, I felt comfortable talking to a woman without it sounding like an awkward attempt to chat her up – definitely not my specialist subject! I catch her eye and wave to her in between beats. She smiles, shyly, and waves back.

Another hour goes by, during which we manage to play a few requests and do a couple of encores. I'm beginning to feel we've just about exhausted our repertoire. Looking around, I'm sensing we've all had enough; even Keith's previous enthusiasm to promote "his" band seems to have evaporated. As the number we're playing reaches its last chord, Marcus signals to us to close the show with a flourish and a bow. As the audience claps and cheers, Keith grabs a mike to make an announcement. 'Thank you, thank you, you're all far too kind. It really has been a whole lot of fun for us to get back together again for Ali's birthday. Now, before you thirsty lot head back to the bar, I have one more, secret, surprise in store for my darling wife. I'm not going to tell you what it is now, you'll just have to trust me, but if you make your way down to the lake at midnight, there's something I'd like to share with you before this special day is over.' He puts a finger up to his lips to emphasise the secret. 'Even Ali doesn't know about it.'

I look at my watch; it's eleven-fifteen. Steve and Ali seem pretty relaxed, but Marco and Keith look exhausted. As for me, I'm soaked in sweat and need a shower. I grab one of the beers that have been sent over and make my way through the dispersing crowd to find Sam.

'Wow!' she says, 'that was amazing. You guys are really good. You didn't tell me you were so talented!' I smile, bashfully, and finish my beer in one long gulp.

'Listen, I need to take a shower. Will you wait for me here?'

She thinks for a moment. 'No, I'll come with you if that's okay. I've been standing here on my own a while. Besides, I like talking to you.' She slips her arm through mine and we make our way up to my room.

While I jump in the shower, Samantha sits in a small armchair, leafing through a glossy magazine. As I rinse off the soap, it suddenly dawns on me that my clean clothes are in the bedroom, which means I'm going to have to go in and find them or ask her to hand me something to wear. Being, I admit, a bit overweight and not likely to be mistaken for Mr Universe, I'm reluctant to wrap a towel around myself and parade in front of her. On the other hand, it seems a bit childish of me to ask her to sort out some clothes. As if she's been reading my mind, Sam taps on the bathroom door while I'm drying myself. 'Dave,' she enquires, 'do you want me to hand you some clothes?'

I hesitate for a moment. 'Er, no, no, that's okay. I'm coming out.' Pulling in my stomach and wrapping the towel tightly around my now reduced waist, I take a deep breath and head into the bedroom, avoiding eye contact with Sam.

She starts to giggle. 'Gosh,' she says, 'I hardly know him and already I'm in the drummer's bedroom and he's got no clothes on. Anybody would think I'm some kind of groupie!' Gripping the towel firmly with one hand, I swiftly pull out a fresh shirt and a pair of trousers from the wardrobe, scooping up some clean pants in the process. As I turn to walk back towards the bathroom, I give a kind of apologetic look to Sam, who continues to stand and smile, not saying a word. Just as I make it to the door, I manage to step on a corner of the bath towel. The bloody thing descends around my ankles as I tumble, bare-arsed, into the bathroom. This time, I can hear friendly amusement in her voice as she calls out, 'That wasn't exactly rock 'n' roll, was it?'

A few minutes later, I emerge, feeling refreshed and more at ease. I move towards Samantha, who is looking out of the open window. She turns towards me, tilts her head and kisses me on the lips. 'Better?' she says.

I put my arms around her and smile into her eyes. 'Much better, thanks.' We remain holding each other tightly, swaying gently to the music drifting up from the marquee. A mild panic floats into my brain, thinking that this situation might lead to sex and wondering if I packed the helpful pills I was prescribed after my prostate op; pills that I've had very little use for, or practice with, up till now.

'So, what's the big secret?' she asks. 'What's happening at midnight?'

'Ah, well,' I say, my mind coming back to the present, 'Keith wanted a grand finale for Ali's birthday, so he's organised a massive firework display.' I glance at my watch; it's nearly ten to twelve. 'We'd better get going if you don't want to miss the start.'

Sam turns to look out of the window. 'Why don't we watch from up here? We can see the lake, so we should have the perfect view. Besides,' she adds, stroking my back, 'I think it's rather romantic, don't you?'

'That's a lovely idea,' I say. 'I'll nip downstairs and find us a couple of drinks before it starts.'

'That's an even better idea,' she replies. I rush down the stairs two at a time and find the bar deserted. In a moment of inspiration, I grab a bottle of champagne from the ice bucket and a couple of glasses and run back up the stairs, just in time to hear the first burst of fireworks through the open window. I pour the champagne; we toast each other and lean against the windowsill, enjoying the display. Burst after burst roars into the night sky, the glittering performance reflected in the waters of the lake. I have to admit it looks bloody impressive. *Well done, Keith*, I think.

The rockets are shooting into the air with increasing frequency and loudness, and I guess we must be coming to the climax of the show as one firework climbs into the sky and explodes in a massive burst of shimmering colours. As the flashes light up the sky and the echo of explosions rolls around in the night air, I realise I can hear another noise: the unmistakable sound of sirens. I turn to look at Sam. 'Can you hear that?'

'Yes,' she nods. 'Do you think it's a fire engine? Maybe one of the fireworks has set fire to something.'

I peer out of the window to see if I can detect any flames or smoke but there's nothing obvious in view. Then I notice the flashing blue lights bouncing off the white walls of the marquee. As I lean further out of the window, I see two ambulances pull up at the corner of the house. Moments later, a quartet of medics starts rushing through the dispersing crowd towards the lake. *Jesus*, I think, *there must have been some kind of accident.* I grab Sam. 'Come on,' I say, 'we'd better get down there. You're a doctor, you might be useful.' I realise she's told me she's a psychiatrist but, I think to myself, she's been to med school; she must still know the basics. As we make our way against the flow of departing guests, I notice that some of them are looking more serious than you'd imagine at the end of a firework display. Margo and Naomi pass us by, clutching each other, looking distressed. As we get nearer to the lake, I can see a small knot of people gathered at the edge. I can make out the figures of Marcus and Steve. Steve has his hands to his face; Marco's are laced together behind his head. Ali seems to be holding on to Gloria, her head buried into Gloria's neck, sobbing. As we reach the disturbing scene, and before I can say anything, I notice the medics kneeling over the prone figure of a man. At first, I can't make out who it is, then I see his face – oh my God, it's Keith! I edge over towards Marcus. 'Jesus Christ, what happened?'

He pulls me towards him. He looks dazed, shaking his head. 'One minute we're all watching the fireworks, Keith's clapping and cheering like a kid, the next minute the poor bugger's collapsed on the ground, just as the show was finishing.' I don't know what to say; all I can do is look at Keith lying motionless. Now I see Samantha kneeling next to one of the paramedics. They exchange a few words, then she looks at me, slowly shaking her head; the look on her face says, *I'm so sorry*.

An hour later, we're sitting around the kitchen table trying to piece together what happened. Ali is upstairs, comforting Sophie and Jake and the grandchildren. Fortunately, they were all standing on the pool terrace for the display and hadn't seen Keith collapse. The ambulance crew have taken Keith's body away; I'm guessing there will need to be a post-mortem. A pot of coffee and a bottle of cognac are on the table, and everyone has helped themselves to whichever they need the most. Marcus has been great, ushering the guests back to their cars and the minivans that had been laid on to take them home. He's asked the catering people to pack up quietly and leave anything that's not urgent. He's even managed to have a word with Keith's estate manager, to make sure the staff are aware and suggest they take the next day off. The way Marcus describes what happened, everyone was laughing and enjoying the firework display, oohing and ahhing with each loud, colourful burst. Ali was holding on to Keith's waist; he'd always known she had a childlike pleasure in watching a big firework display. Then, without anyone noticing, and as the explosions were getting louder and louder, Keith had lurched forward and slid out of the arms of Ali and fallen onto the grass. It was only when Ali began screaming Keith's name that people close by realised that something was not right. As it became obvious that Keith was not getting up, as Ali knelt beside him frantically trying to loosen his bow tie, first one, then several mobile phones were being pulled from pockets to call for an ambulance. (We later learned the emergency services had received nearly fifty phone calls requesting help from the same location. At first, they'd thought it must be a major incident before realising it was all in aid of one person.) One of the guests had tried to use his knowledge of resuscitation but without any obvious success, although he'd kept trying until the first paramedic arrived. While all this was happening, the display had reached its finale and most of the guests had begun to turn back towards the house, unaware of the scene that was unfolding. Only those close by had begun to realise that the evening had come to a tragic end.

It's 2am by the time anyone thinks about going to bed. Steve has been talking about staying on to be with Ali, although I know he and Gloria have a flight booked on Monday to get back to their kids in Spain. Margo and Naomi are going to try and get some sleep then head back to Marco's flat in town later in the morning. Marcus reckons he'll stay for the rest of the day until he knows what Ali wants to do. I realise I've been holding on to Sam's hand under the table. I look at her with a questioning look, as if to say, *What do you want to do?*, knowing that her car is here and maybe she's thinking of driving home. As the others slowly get up from the table and make their way towards their bedrooms, she gives my hand a squeeze. 'Come on,' she says, 'I think we should go to bed, too.'

TWENTY-SEVEN

ALISON

I open my eyes, slowly. My eyelids are glued together with the make-up I hadn't bothered to remove and the tears I'd shed with Sophie and Jack. I'm lying on top of my bed looking down at the clothes I'd been too weary to take off. The bright sunshine pouring through the uncurtained window hurts my eyes; it seems to be mocking the dark events of the night before. 'Come on!' it's saying, 'get up, can't you see it's another beautiful day?' I pull the bedcover up to my chin, seeking comfort. Part of me wants to pretend that nothing happened, that it was all a dream, but it's too late for that. I have to accept that Keith has gone. *Poor Keith*, I think, *what a way for you to go; what a silly way, watching a bloody firework display.*

I don't remember too much about what happened after he collapsed. It felt like I was sleepwalking, people moving around me, saying things I couldn't hear. It was only when I saw the ambulance lady shaking her head that I realised that Keith was already dead. Of course, I'd known about his heart condition. I was the one who'd nagged him to go to the doctor a couple of years ago when he'd had a "funny turn" shouting at his beloved football team on TV. He'd tried to tell me it was nothing and only agreed to go if I didn't tell anyone. Even when he'd been told by the doctor, and then a consultant, that his blood pressure was too high, that he should consider changing his lifestyle, he continued to dismiss their advice, only saying he would try to "get home from the office a bit earlier and cut down on the red wine". But he didn't. He continued to run his empire with all his usual enthusiasm, despite my efforts to get him to take things more easily, although he did notice we'd begun to eat healthier meals at home, something he said just went to prove he was "making an effort". He made me promise not to say anything to anyone, especially the children; he didn't want people making a fuss, and besides, it would "send out the wrong signals" in his business world. So, I stopped nagging him. And no, I'm not shocked or surprised.

A thousand thoughts tumble through my head, each one surfacing to be swiftly replaced by another. What about the children? What about Keith's business? What about this house? Keith had never really included me in either his, or our, financial affairs. Whenever I asked him how we could afford things, he always winked and told me not to "worry about money". I think he always liked the idea of providing for me, something he'd promised to do ever since we got engaged. I suppose I got complacent and, I admit, I got used to buying whatever I needed, although I'd never say I was an extravagant person. What about our friends? What do I tell them? What about the funeral? I decide the best decision is to make no decision, except take a shower and get dressed. Even that simple task presents its own dilemma. Should I be wearing something black? Should I make an appearance as the grieving widow? At least the shower is making me feel more awake. I stand under the hot, powerful stream, thinking how nice it would be just to stay here for the rest of the day. In the end, I decide this is not the day to be wearing black. I opt, instead, for a simple summer dress and style my hair into a loose ponytail. Looking at my watch, the beautiful and no doubt very expensive watch Keith gave me one birthday, I decide it's time to go downstairs and face people.

I'm used to entering a room without expecting anyone to stop talking; family or guests. This morning is different. As soon as I appear in the kitchen, I sense an immediate lull in the conversation. Marcus sees me first and walks towards me. 'Ali,' he says, softly, and puts his arms around me. 'How're you doing? Did you manage to get any sleep?' I smile weakly as if to say yes, but not a lot. 'Come and sit down, let me get you a coffee,' he says, steering me towards the big table. I see Steve and Gloria, Dave and Samantha, the remnants of breakfast in front of them. Looking at their concerned faces, I find it impossible to prevent a tear rolling down my cheek.

Steve stands and comes over, squatting next to me, stroking my hand. 'Hey, Sis, it's okay. Cry if you want to.'

I sniff, once, dabbing my nose on a napkin, and stroke his hair. 'I'm okay, really. I'll be fine.' The mood in the room seems to relax. This should have been a typical Sunday morning-after-the-party breakfast. Hungover people devouring a fry-up and going over the hilarious, and possibly scandalous, events of the night before. Only this time, Keith's not here to make his usual blustering fuss about the behaviour of "some of those awful people".

'Has anyone seen the children?' I ask, attempting to make some kind of conversation.

Sam smiles. 'Jake came down a little while ago and made some breakfast for the kids. He took it back upstairs.'

'So,' I say, 'what are you all going to do now? Will you be staying? I mean, we were supposed to be having a big lunch, there's loads of food.' The thought of such an arrangement suddenly sounds ridiculous in the circumstances and I burst into tears. 'I'm sorry,' I muffle into the napkin I realise I've been twisting around in my hand, 'this is such a bloody mess. I have no idea what I'm supposed to do.'

Marcus pulls a chair over and sits down next to me. 'Listen, Ali, this has been a terrible shock for all of us, especially you.' He's holding my hand, stroking my arm. 'We've been having a chat and come up with a few ideas. Gloria has to get back to Cunit, but Steve is going to stay here with you, at least for the time being. Dave and Sam are going to head off this morning, although she has offered to cook a lunch if you'd like that. I've had a brief chat with Jake this morning. He knows the ropes at the office so I've suggested he call a meeting of all the directors. They can meet here tomorrow and work out a statement for a press release about Keith before the markets get wind of his...' he pauses '...passing. How does that sound?'

I give him a weak smile and squeeze his hand. 'Thanks, Marcus, sounds like you've got everything under control. But what about you, what are you going to do?'

'Well,' he replies, 'Margo and Naomi need to get back to Zurich so I'm going to take them to the airport later and then come back here to keep Steve company. I also suggested to Jake I sit in on his meeting tomorrow, maybe help with drafting the press release.' He smiles. 'I used to write copy, if you remember.'

The thought of Marcus being around to help Jake and Steve fills me with an enormous sense of relief, knowing that I can face the next few days without having to make a load of decisions on my own. Surrounded by such good friends, I begin to relax for the first time this morning. 'Any chance of some toast and another coffee?' I ask, politely.

'Look, my darlings, it's very sweet of you to want to stay with me but I'll be fine, honestly. Besides, your Uncle Steve is going to stay with me and Marcus is going to be here for a few days, too.' When I explained to them about their father's heart condition, Jake, understandably, was angry that he didn't know about it, as if he could have done something to prevent it! Sophie was much calmer, realising that this was just the sort of decision she would have expected from her father; someone who would never have wanted his children to worry about him. 'I think you should take the children home today and call me this evening. There's going to be a lot to sort out and I'm going to need your help with that. Anyway, I'll see you tomorrow, Jake, when you have your meeting.' They both, reluctantly, agree, and after lots of hugs and kisses, I stand in the driveway and wave them off.

I wander into the garden and sit on the wooden bench overlooking the pool, trying to gather my thoughts. The obvious signs of the night before are still there. The empty marquee, tables and chairs piled up in stacks, a line of vases filled with flowers that decorated the tables, here and there an empty glass or bottle, an indication that the caterers had left early, as politely requested. Looking across the vast lawn towards the lake, my eye is drawn towards a colourful object lying on the grass close to where Keith collapsed. I get up and walk towards it, curious. As I bend to pick it up, I realise it's the remnants of a firework, a rocket, its stick still attached. On the charred label I can just make out the words *GIANT FINALE*. *How fucking ironic,* I think to myself, snapping the stick in two. I turn around and look back at the house, its honey-coloured stone bathed in sunlight, looking solid, permanent. As far as the house is concerned, the events of last night are just one of the many occasions, good and sad, it must have witnessed over hundreds of years. Standing there, feeling the grass beneath my feet, it finally dawns on me that my life is about to change. I mean, this house for a start. Yes, it's incredibly beautiful, but do I feel it's my home? For Keith, it was always more about status than somewhere to live. It's nothing like the place we lived in when we were first married, or the house where the children grew up; those are what I think of as real homes. I can't imagine what it will be like rattling around on my own in so many empty rooms.

I walk slowly back to the bench, enjoying the warm sun on my bare shoulders. The sound of glasses clinking on a tray interrupts my thoughts. Sam sits next to me, puts the tray on the grass and pours out two drinks. 'I thought you might like something,' she says, handing me a glass. 'This is my special sparkling elderflower, with a drop of gin added. Thought it might help.'

'Thanks, Sam,' I say, "that's really sweet of you, and thanks for hanging on, too.'

She squeezes my hand. 'Don't be silly, I couldn't just leave. Besides, I've got a Sunday roast on the go.'

I turn to look at my friend from our days at uni; the one, I must admit, I haven't seen often enough. I put my arms around her and give her a big hug. 'So, what about you and Dave? All a bit sudden, isn't it?'

She smiles. 'All a bit unexpected if you ask me. But I really like him. He's been so thoughtful and kind. It's been a long time since I met someone I felt was on the same page as me.'

I give her a reassuring pat on the arm. 'I've known Dave a long time and I can tell you he's someone you can rely on. He's a really lovely guy, good drummer too.' We sit for a while lost in our own thoughts until a sudden breeze sends ripples across the lake.

'I ought to get back to check on the roast,' says Sam. 'Shall I leave you on your own for a while?'

I clear the worrying thoughts that have been going around in my head. 'No, I'll walk back with you. I need to be doing something. Let me give you a hand, even if it's only peeling carrots. I think I can manage that! Besides, you won't know where I keep everything in the kitchen.' We make our way back to the house, arms around each other, as we might have done forty years ago.

TWENTY-EIGHT

2008 – JAKE

Even if I say so myself, Dad's funeral went pretty well. It took a bit of organising, especially as I'd been thrown in at the deep end with the business as well, but Mum and Uncle Steve and Sophie really stepped up to the mark. I don't think I could have done it without them.

Obviously, everyone was in a state of shock the night he died, although I can't help thinking he would have appreciated bowing out with the sound of loud fireworks ringing in everyone's ears. To the outside world, it would have seemed quite typical for him to be the centre of attention, but I knew him, first and foremost, as a dad, someone who liked nothing more than just hanging out with his children and, later, his grandkids.

I remember one summer holiday, I think we were in Spain, and he decided to take me out in a rowing boat – not just a row around the bay but out into what seemed to me like the ocean. I must have been about seven or eight and happy to sit in the stern, hands on bare, brown knees, watching him pull on the oars singing *A Life on the Ocean Wave* at the top of his voice. This was all in the days before life jackets or health and safety. I think his plan was to row along the coast to the beach to where we'd left Mum and Sophie. Looking back, it was a typical example of his attitude to life, being impulsive while having fun; risky maybe, but he made me feel completely safe. Mind you, I'm pretty sure he got a bollocking when we eventually got home; me tired, him probably exhausted, but I'd loved the whole adventure.

To be honest, when he first suggested I work for him, I wasn't too keen. When I left uni, I wanted to go travelling, do my own thing, while he was eager to get me into one of his companies to "learn the ropes". We had a huge argument about that, but eventually, with a bit of persuasion from Mum, he relented, but only on the condition I start working for him after one year away. Having got that sorted, he then gave me a travel card loaded with a thousand quid – that was so typical of Dad, always generous after he'd made his point.

The day Marcus organised a meeting of the main board just after Dad died was a bit nerve-racking for everyone. Fifteen people sat around the dining table looking strangely unbusinesslike in their casual clothes. Most of them had been at the party so they knew what had happened. Like most boards of directors, they were suspicious about why Marcus, an outsider, was there. But he proved to be a skilful chair of the meeting. Having got the first item on the agenda – a press release that he had prepared the night before – agreed, we soon moved on to the main business – who was going to replace Dad as CEO? Up to that point in time, I'd been running one of the online subsidiaries, so I wasn't on the main board. It helped that I'd graduated with a degree in IT, because looking around the room I suspected most of them only used their computers for sending emails. It made me realise that while I didn't have their experience, I would be a lot more savvy when it came to matters concerning technology. After much polite discussion, understandable expressions of concern mixed with genuine words of condolence, it was moved and approved that I be invited to join the main board with a brief to "watch and learn". An interim CEO was appointed to steady the ship and send a message of confidence to the City. As the meeting concluded, it was generally understood that I was the "heir apparent", especially as Mum, Sophie and myself were destined to inherit Dad's majority shareholding. But it was made clear I was going to have to prove myself to this hard-headed bunch of business people.

It took a few weeks to organise the funeral. There'd had to be a post-mortem to confirm the cause of death – a waste of time according to Mum, who knew straight away what had happened. Looking back, I suppose Soph and I were pretty shocked, as we'd never really thought of Dad being "ill", but I guess some of the signs were there. I wish we'd done more to get him to slow down, but he probably would have laughed and told us he was as fit as a flea, while pouring himself another glass of his favourite burgundy.

Mum dithered about where to have the funeral but eventually decided to hold it at the local church in the village. It wouldn't be convenient for everyone wanting to pay their respects, and there wasn't much in the way of parking, but it was in a beautiful setting and, despite the fact we weren't what you'd call regular churchgoers, the vicar turned out to be a really friendly chap, sympathetic and efficient. He helped us choose a couple of popular hymns, the kind most people know the tune and the words to, and advised us on the most appropriate prayers. Mum decided she wanted to ask the church choir to sing one of Dad's favourite hymns, *Jerusalem*; she said it would be "uplifting" for everyone, filling the small church with its patriotic words and lusty tune. I must admit I was finding it all a bit *Last Night of the Proms*, but she was determined to have it. She also chose the music to accompany the coffin into the church, one of Elgar's Variations played on the organ, then Ry Cooder's beautiful instrumental, *I Think It's Going To Work Out Fine*, as the coffin was carried out. We'd already decided to have a family-only cremation the day after the service; it was too much to organise everyone getting from the church to the crematorium. Besides, as the vicar gently explained, the church only offered a burial to its "regular customers".

Marcus was a real help sorting out the public announcement of Dad's death and sending out emails with all the details of the funeral, and it was an easy decision to hold the wake back at Mum and Dad's house. Most people had been there for the party so knew how to find it, and it was a simple job to convert one of the paddocks into a temporary car park. We even employed the same caterers and had the marquee re-erected in case the weather changed on the day. It was a great relief when the sun shone brilliantly all day long.

The church had been packed with people; it was standing room only. I'm sure the villagers who watched the hearse arriving, followed by so many cars, must have wondered who the celebrity was who was having his funeral in their church. Even the vicar mentioned to me afterwards what a real pleasure it had been for him to see so many people filling his church. I think he would have preferred it if it had been for a wedding and not a funeral, but he was too polite to say so.

There'd been so many people who'd asked if they could say something about Dad during the service, evidence of the warmth and respect they felt towards him. In the end, we had to restrict it to half a dozen; otherwise, we'd have been there all afternoon. One of Dad's directors, a chap who'd worked with him almost from the start of his career, recalled how Dad had been a real entrepreneur, coping with the ups and downs of creating a business empire, always encouraging people to come up with fresh ideas, never afraid to take a risk. Several heads were nodding and smiling, even those who might have been considered his rivals in business. Marcus made a charming, light-hearted speech that had the whole church laughing as he recounted what happened on Dad's stag night and how his struggle to learn the chords of a tune never got in the way of his enthusiasm to get the band more gigs. After Marcus, practically the whole congregation was reduced to tears as Ruby, Sophie's seven-year-old daughter, stood up, her head just above the lectern, and told everyone how much she loved her grandpapa and how she was going to miss him teaching her to swim and showing her how to tell the time.

As I said, the funeral went pretty well.

Almost a year later, Mum, Sophie and I were having a quiet drink when the subject came up of what to do with Dad's ashes. They'd been delivered to Mum, in a surprisingly heavy cardboard box, a few days after the cremation, and she'd been keeping them ever since in a cupboard in the garage. Not out of disrespect, although I don't think she was too keen on having them in the house, but, she reasoned, she thought "he" might prefer to be near his vintage E-type Jag, the one he'd spent a fortune having restored. It was still sitting in the garage; Mum hadn't wanted to sell it before we'd sorted out what to do with the ashes. It was Sophie who came up with a brilliant idea. She'd done some research on the web and found out you could have the ashes packed into a firework, a fucking big rocket, that could shoot several hundred feet into the air. Mum and I both loved the idea. It seemed the perfect solution and, given the circumstances of his death, the most splendid way to finish the display he'd planned for Mum's birthday. And so, on the anniversary of his death, the whole family, plus Marcus, Dave and Samantha – Uncle Steve and Gloria couldn't make it as she was touring – gathered at the edge of the lake as soon as it got dark. With our glasses filled with champagne, my eldest boy, Toby, was given the honour of lighting the fuse. For a moment, all we could see was the glowing touch paper then, with an enormous whoosh, the rocket took off into the night sky. We watched it climb for several seconds until we couldn't crane our necks any further. Then it exploded with a massive bang, lighting up the sky with the most beautiful starburst. We clapped and cheered and raised our glasses and watched as the colours slowly fell back to earth and faded into the night. I couldn't help imagining Dad, watching over us as we stood below, while his ashes settled, like a fine dust, over his estate. I'm pretty sure he would have appreciated the symbolism of the moment.

So, here I am, setting off for the office. It's early on a beautiful summer morning – I like to get going before the traffic builds on the motorway. I nudge the Bentley onto the slip road and accelerate gently, feeling the satisfying surge of power beneath my right foot. Did I mention the Bentley? Frankly, I think I deserve it after the deal I did selling our online business to one of the big US search engines. It was a bit hairy at times, but I managed to convince them they were getting a huge, loyal customer base and impeccable goodwill. The expensive car is my reward to myself. I think Dad would have been really chuffed, proud too, although knowing him, he would probably wind me up for not buying a Jag.

TWENTY-NINE

2010 – MARCUS

When I told Alison I wanted to have a retirement party, she laughed. 'What do you mean, a retirement party? You haven't had a proper job for years. What, exactly, are you retiring from?' She was on a roll now. 'Who are you going to invite to this party? All your old workmates? As far as I know, you've been working, if you can call it that, by yourself for ages.' It's true, I haven't had a "proper" job since the mobile phone company bought my song for their world-wide TV commercials and the royalties came rolling in, although they'd dried up a long time ago.

'Well,' I said, pretending to sound quite hurt by her accusation, 'I've been doing bits and pieces, you know, keeping my hand in with the jingles, doing the odd bit of copywriting, stuff like that.'

'Exactly.' She smiles. 'You've had the life of Riley, as far as I can tell. So, tell me, what's this all about? Is it an age thing?'

Maybe it is. I'm past sixty, still feeling pretty fit, but wondering if my career, such as it is, has come to a grinding halt. I'd be the first to admit I've never been that ambitious; you could say I'm a bit of a lazy sod. Actually, lazy is the wrong word. I've never been afraid of hard work, but I've never felt the urge to really push myself. I could blame my generation: the baby boomers. Born towards the end of the war, raised on free orange juice and cod liver oil, fed into an education system that still believed in the "Three R's", divided by the dreaded eleven-plus exam – which I managed to pass, much to the surprise of my teachers and, if they were being totally honest, my parents – then trotting along to the brand new grammar school conveniently built ten minutes from home, proudly wearing my blazer and cap, where I spent the next seven years lapping up the subjects I liked, geography and sport, while basically being bored by anything else. Most of my school reports would say, *Could do better if he applied himself.* So, it was no real surprise to me when I left with five O levels, one of which I'm proud to say was woodwork, and one A level in, you guessed it, geography. Not exactly university material. Did I mention I was awarded my school colours for playing in the first XI and first XV? Of the few words the headmaster ever spoke to me – apart from saying 'This has been long overdue' as I bent over his chair while he gave me six of the best – the most memorable were, 'Keep up the rugby.' Hardly what you'd call encouraging career advice. But then there was no shortage of jobs in the early sixties. Britain was booming and anyone with half a brain and capable of stringing a few sentences together could find work. With my one A level, I managed to get a job with a large insurance company as a trainee underwriter. I had visions of becoming a member of Lloyds within at least two years. Then a mate said there was a vacancy in his advertising agency for a trainee copywriter, and it sounded a lot more glamorous than writing insurance policies. So, I swapped insurance for advertising, starting at eight pounds a week, and I loved it. Turned out I was pretty good at it, too. I was soon promoted from trainee, swapped agencies a couple of times, earnt good money and still managed to turn out for the rugby team and play in the band at weekends. Compared to today, there was still an air of innocence. It was the age of "flower power", where everyone wanted to be "laid back". Our soundtrack was The Beatles, The Beach Boys, The Small Faces, Procol Harum, The Stones. Girls went on the pill, so they could have sex without fear of getting pregnant. Boys didn't think about wearing a "johnny". Everyone seemed to be shagging everyone else without fear of disease; that would come years later. Our drugs were nothing harder than cigarettes and alcohol; only a few "hot heads" experimented with pot or acid.

Don't let anyone ever tell you the sixties weren't a great time to be young. Let me give you a wonderful example. Imagine you're twenty-one, you've rented a cruiser on the Thames with two of your best mates for the weekend, you've each got your current girlfriend on board, it's mid-summer and you're floating down the river with *A Whiter Shade of Pale* blasting out of the portable cassette player. You've got a beer in one hand and a Gitanes in the other. Your girlfriend, who has just returned from her package holiday to Lloret de Mar sporting a gorgeous tan, is wearing possibly the shortest skirt in the world and sending you a suggestive smile as she crosses her legs to reveal a flash of white knickers, and you know, later in that cramped cabin, you're going to have the best sex ever. Now I know what you're thinking, this all sounds like a young man's sexual fantasy, but believe me, it really happened. Her name was Fiona; I often wonder whatever happened to her. As I was saying, we were the baby boomers; we were a lucky generation.

'An age thing?' I reply. 'Give me a break. I'm only sixty-five!'

'Well, what is it?' she asks. 'Have you got some mystery illness you haven't told me about, or are you just a teeny bit bored?' I can hear her turning over on the bunk above me. She says she gets claustrophobic if she has to sleep on the lower bunk. We're on the car ferry to St Malo, having decided to drive to Suzette via an overnight stop with friends of Ali's who live in Rochefort. We keep an old Renault at the house for local errands, but sometimes it's nice to take a day or two to drive there, plus there's the added bonus of filling the boot with loads of booze to take back.

I lie back in the darkness of the cabin. 'Not bored, really, just think it would be nice to have a party. I thought retirement would be a good excuse. Maybe we should call it an engagement party instead.'

I can sense the smile in her muffled reply. 'Don't start that again, Marcus. Go to sleep.' It's true, the "M" word has surfaced from time to time, but neither of us is in any hurry to make our relationship "official". Anyway, I've never been married and I see no reason to do it now. I came closest with the French girl, Monique, but she was ambitious and would never have stayed in London. I, on the other hand, am too settled in my ways. I'm happy in my own company, which is another way of saying I'm probably quite selfish when it comes to making a commitment to a relationship. Not that I haven't been in love before, although it can be easy to confuse lust with love. As for Alison, the legal complications would be too much of a headache. Keith left her a wealthy woman and there's no way I'd want to come between her kids and their inheritance. I've got my money and she's got hers and we're content to leave it like that. But, from time to time, I like to tease her by suggesting we do the right thing and get hitched, a suggestion she has politely, but rudely, declined.

After Keith died, Alison would come up to town from time to time to go shopping or see a movie, and so it was convenient for her to stay at my flat, although she could have easily booked herself into a hotel. To be honest, it didn't take very long before we were sleeping together, although we made sure we were very discreet about it, not wishing to upset her children. It was clear that our feelings for each other hadn't changed since the episode in Suzette, but neither of us had been prepared to admit it or take it further. There was no way Alison was going to start an affair while she was still married to Keith; she would have thought that was far too "grubby". But the funeral was more than two years ago and we've been together now for over a year. At the beginning, I would spend a few days at a time at the house in Sussex, or she would come and stay with me in town. Jake and Sophie, of course, were soon aware of the situation, but in fairness they took it pretty well. I think they are both adult enough to know we weren't disrespecting their father and, even if they wouldn't admit it, they were probably relieved that someone was taking care of their mother. Besides, I like her children and I think they genuinely like me. When Alison decided, eventually, to sell the property – she really didn't need such a vast place or the hassle of keeping it going – she said she'd rather come and live with me in London than buy another house in the country. It seemed a decision based more on romance than practicality, my bachelor flat not really being suitable for two people, no matter how much we like each other, which is why we are on our way to the house in Suzette; somewhere we've been spending more and more of our time, a place where we both feel more relaxed.

I can't sleep. I rarely sleep on the ferry. People say the hum of the engine or the gentle roll of the boat is enough to help them sleep. I'm not one of those people. I find the noise and movement disturbing, but then, I find it difficult to sleep on planes, too. I'd like to turn on the light and read but I don't want to disturb Ali. Her rhythmic breathing tells me she's already asleep: a talent she has that I find slightly frustrating. Instead, I start to think about who I might invite to my party.

Despite my grumbles about sleeping on boats, planes, etc., I must have fallen asleep as I'm woken by the god-awful, faux Celtic music coming over the PA system, something I've discovered from previous trips is impossible to switch off. The cheery announcer tells us breakfast is being served in the restaurant – at half past bloody six in the morning! Alison turns on the light, swings a leg over the side of her bunk, descends the ladder and squeezes into my bed. As we cuddle up, she reaches down to grip my morning-hard penis and suggests, in the sweetest possible way, that a quickie would be a nicer way to start the day than breakfast. Giggling and trying our best not to fall out of the bunk, we make love, urgently, rapidly. It's one of the many things I've learnt to love about her – her sense of spontaneous fun, something she admits she lost for many years.

It's still early by the time we leave the port, so we head to Dinan where we know there's a café that serves just about the best coffee and croissants. 'So, have you decided who you're going to invite to this party of yours?' says Ali, licking her finger and sweeping up the few crumbs of pastry left on the plate. 'I mean, where are all these work chums you've been hiding? Are you going to invite them to Suzette?' She has a point. Having gone through a few names during the night, I've come to the conclusion there's only a handful of people, other than close friends and family, I'd want to invite. And whether they'd be prepared to travel to Provence is another matter altogether.

'Okay,' I concede, 'maybe the idea of a party is not so great. Perhaps a "gathering" is a better suggestion. We could invite all the kids, the grandchildren, Dave and Sam, Steve and Gloria and their lot, you know?'

She drains her coffee and smiles. 'You mean more like a reunion?'

'Well, yes,' I say, 'if you put it like that.'

She looks out of the window, mulling over something, then turns and strokes my hand. 'I think it's a lovely idea, sweetheart, but please don't turn it into a band reunion. We've had enough disasters at those, thank you very much.' She's right, of course. Getting the band together again is an event we can leave in the past.

As it turned out, we never did arrange that party. After our detour to Rochefort, we spent the rest of summer tootling around Suzette. Our days were spent swimming, playing the occasional game of tennis, when Alison would invariably beat me easily, exploring the wonderful food markets that still exist in rural France, Sundays at the flea market in Carpentras, taking advantage of the Côtes du Rhône vineyards practically on our doorstep, or simply soaking up the sun by the pool. If it sounds idyllic, it was. We'd become very happy and content with each other, and it was clear we didn't need a party to celebrate our life together.

Of course, we still had visitors, plenty of them. Typically, Jake would charter a private jet and fly down with his family and bring Sophie's as well. He really is a chip off the old Keith block, never off the phone, wheeling and dealing. They would usually stay for a week; it was lovely to see them, but exhausting. We would both breath a sigh of relief as we waved their plane down the runway.

Margo and Naomi arrived by car for a few days in August, bringing my grandson with them. Grandson; now there's a word I never expected to hear. I knew they always wanted to have a child, although I didn't know which option they would choose. Between them, they decided Naomi would bear a child from one of Margo's eggs, fertilised by a donor they selected from a sperm bank found on the internet. All very twenty-first century! We'd had several discussions over the phone about what his name would be, although I always said it was their choice as long as he wasn't named after me. After Marcus and Margo, I figured there might be enough "Ms" in the family. In the end, they decided to call him Georges, a kind of Swiss/English mash-up. He's nearly two now and delightful. Seeing the three of them together, it amazes me that anyone could think that a child has to have a "mother" and a "father". Naomi and Margo have a beautiful, loving relationship with Georges, and I'm sure he'll grow up to be a respectful young man, an example to some of my generation, I can tell you. Since he arrived, Ali and I have become like two doting grandparents, although I put my foot down when it came to deciding what I would be called. Vanity alone decreed I was not going to be "Grandad" or "Grandpa", not at "my age". I don't think Ali was too keen, either; besides, she had her own grandchildren who always called her "Mimi". After several attempts, we came up with "Opi", meaning Older Person, which I rather liked and which, increasingly, I am known as by all the grandchildren, not to mention their parents, too, who find it an amusing way to refer to me.

One evening, sipping pastis with Margo while Naomi puts Georges to bed, she tells me they're going to have another baby. Ali comes out from the kitchen carrying a bowl of salad and wonders why we're smiling. When I tell her the news, she gives Margo a huge hug. 'Congratulations!' she says, nodding in my direction, 'here's one old man who is going to be very happy.' Just at that moment, Naomi appears on the patio. Glancing at Margo, she smiles shyly, then sits on Margo's lap, realising that we too know about their baby plans.

It's early September, the sun streaming into the bedroom, still warm. I'm awake and looking at Ali next to me, still asleep. Her dark hair spread across the pillow shows not a trace of grey; her face is almost wrinkle-free. To my eyes, admittedly without my glasses, she still looks about twenty. I turn towards her and put my arm across her shoulder. She stirs, opening one eye. 'Good morning,' I say, kissing her nose.

'Morning,' she replies, sleepily, offering no further words, but inching her body towards me.

'I've been thinking,' I say, 'how about we go and see Steve? It's been a while since we've seen him and Gloria. Why don't you phone him this morning? We could easily get to Cunit in a day from here.'

Alison sits up and takes a sip of water. 'You mean you want to go tomorrow?'

'Why not? There's nothing stopping us. We're free agents, go where we like when we like.'

'Okay. I'll call him later, but you're going to have to make me breakfast first,' she says, nudging me in the ribs and pulling the duvet up to her chin. 'It's your punishment for waking me up.'

A couple of days later, we're on the motorway to Spain, singing along to some early Bob Dylan on the CD player. We arrive in Cunit just as the sun is setting and decide to park the car and walk to the beach before going to Steve and Gloria's house. The village is almost unrecognisable from the sleepy place we arrived at forty years ago. Then it was a dusty, rural dot on the map that just happened to be next to the sea. It was more than an hour's drive to Barcelona or a slow ride on the local train that stopped, once a day, at the wooden platform that served as the station. Now the village had developed into a suburb of Barcelona, populated by professionals who enjoy the benefit of an express train service into work and the beach on their doorstep. Ali and I struggle to recognise any of the places we remembered; the bakery, the restaurant, the village square, all now converted into shiny shops. We find a sign pointing to the beach and finally find one thing that hasn't changed: the alleyway under the railway. In those days, it was a simple brick and timber structure supporting the single track; now it's a tiled and brightly lit passageway several metres long, running below the double tracks above. What was once a dusty footpath to the beach is now a paved road. Even the beach has changed. We both have a memory of it being long and wide and almost deserted. Now it seems to have shrunk to a narrow strip, covered in sunbeds and umbrellas. I guess who ever said never go back was right. Rather disappointed, we head back, hand in hand, to Steve's. At least we know his house is in one of the few unspoilt parts of the village. We knock on the door and are greeted by Steve with open arms. He, once the leather-clad, moody guy of few words, is now the happy family man, fetching drinks and chatting away about Gloria's latest tour while he loads the barbecue with chicken which he declares, proudly, is marinated in his own "special sauce". He's put on some weight, which suits him, although still smoking roll-ups, for which Ali gently chides him. But, hey, it's his life and nobody is going to change him now, least of all Gloria.

Later, after we've eaten far too much and drunk a few too many glasses of excellent rioja, Ali wanders across the room and sits down at the electric piano that Steve uses to work on his arrangements for Gloria. She plays for a while, just amusing herself, then I begin to recognise the familiar chords of a song. I look towards her, smiling, and as she reaches the familiar chorus we look at each other and sing, in harmony, "*I got you, babe*".

EPILOGUE

KEITH

When I was alive, I didn't give much thought to death, or dying, but now that I'm up here (I'm assuming "up" and not "down"), it's not too bad at all. I mean, it was a bit of a shock to begin with, finding myself wandering about in daylight when the last thing I remembered was watching the fireworks at midnight on Alison's birthday. I know I should have listened to her and gone to see the doc, but I was always saying, 'Okay, I'll go tomorrow,' so I've only got myself to blame.

If you thought there would be a massive reunion with your parents, grandparents, old friends, chaps from the golf club, etc., forget it. The only people you can see are the ones who got here the same day as you, so it's unlikely you'll know anyone. And everyone's wearing what they died in, so you can imagine there are some bizarre outfits; people walking about in swimsuits, fancy dress, pyjamas, even a few, unfortunate, naked ones. Me, I'm stuck in this bloody dinner suit; I wish I'd changed into something more suitable for summer like the others did.

It did take a while getting used to the fact you lose the power of speech. But on the plus side, you gain the ability to communicate by transferring thoughts. Mind you, there's not a lot of conversation, mainly the odd 'Good day' or 'Hullo' as you pass people strolling about. Actually, I spend most of the time in my "space". It's hard to describe – there's no furniture, like a chair or a bed – but somehow, if I feel like resting, I just close my eyes and imagine the sensation of sitting or lying down. When I open my eyes again, it's still daylight; in fact, there doesn't seem to be any night time at all. The temperature doesn't change, either. It feels like a beautiful, warm, sunny, early June kind of day – every day. There must be a bloody fantastic air con system up here is all I can say. My "'space" doesn't have any walls, either, although when I'm in it, I can't see anyone outside. It feels to me a bit like what it must have felt like to be a monk.

One fantastic feature is the huge screen that seems to materialise, shimmering in front of me as soon as I start thinking about someone who is alive. For example, I'm thinking about Jake at the moment. There he is on his way to work. Looks like he's bought himself a new car, and if I'm not mistaken, it's a Bentley, so he must be having great success at the company – "my" company – he had to take over so unexpectedly. I always knew he could do it, just needed a bit of a prod, although, personally, I would have bought a Jag.

To be honest, I wasn't too keen on seeing my own funeral, but I was pleasantly surprised at how many people came. I didn't know I had so many friends, although I'm guessing some of them were business people, maybe even a few rivals, paying their respects. Unfortunately, the wall screen doesn't allow me to hear people speaking, so I don't actually know what the vicar was saying. I could see Alison sitting in the front row, looking as beautiful as ever, dressed in black. All the family were there, too. I was really touched when Ruby, Sophie's girl, got up to say something; there were a few hankies out at that moment I can tell you. I might have shed a tear myself.

Some while later – I can't say when as there's no sense of time up here. It could have been days or months – I was thinking about Alison and there, on my "screen", I could see her and what looked like the rest of the family down by the lake. You have to understand that it's some way up here, so although I can zoom in, I can't do close-ups, but I get the general picture. All of a sudden, I see this rocket zooming upwards and then exploding in a blaze of colour. It looked fantastic! And in the flash from the bursting firework, I can see the whole of the estate; the house, the pool, the gardens, the fields, lit up like daylight. Absolutely brilliant! Although I keep wondering why only the one rocket? I mean, not what you'd call a real display. Maybe it was someone's birthday.

So, I've been here quite a while now. Every now and then, I tune in to see what's going on down there. Dave and that Samantha he met at the party have moved in together and look extremely happy. Steve and Gloria are still living in Cunit, surrounded by an increasing number of grandchildren ever since she stopped touring. Margo and Naomi dote on their son, and from what I can gather, there's another child on the way. As for Alison, well, she sold the big house; I knew she would, it was never her thing. She and Marcus spend most of their time at the house in Suzette looking for all the world like a very happy couple. It doesn't surprise me; I always knew she fancied him, didn't you? Besides, I'm in no position to go down there and bash him on the nose. Anyway, I always liked Marcus. He was a good pal.

The golden rule in this place is that you can stay as long as there's still someone alive who remembers you. So, I'm relying on the grandchildren to keep me in the picture as long as they hold a memory of me. Up here, they call it "Fading Away". Maybe that's what happens; I'll just fall asleep one sunny day and not wake up again.

After that, who knows?

THANKS

When I began writing this book I didn't appreciate how long it was going to take. I moved house twice; three more grandchildren arrived; I travelled to Italy, France, Spain, Portugal and USA; I lost dear friends and made new ones. Throughout this time, I was grateful for the unfailing support, encouragement and helpful advice from my daughters, Amber and Laura; my best friends, David and Laura Farrant; my golfing pals, Julien, David and Derek; and Renée, the woman who danced into my life.

I thank all of you very much.

Enormous thanks go to the good people at Matador for their friendly, enthusiastic and professional approach to the business of editing and publishing. I would recommend them to any writer.

Thanks also to the village of Cunit – it does exist, although the Bar Estudio, sadly, is no longer there.

Lastly, but by no means least, I would like to send sincere thanks to David, Graham, Martin, Gordon and Dave - the original Alexander's Relations - for giving me the inspiration to start this story.

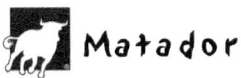

For exclusive discounts on Matador titles,
sign up to our occasional newsletter at
troubador.co.uk/bookshop